She was ... *the phone rang again.*

Elinor hoped whoever it was would give up and go away. But the ringing went on and on. In the end she snatched up the receiver, her voice hoarse and unsteady with fright as she answered. It was Miles, sounding irritable. "I rang several times earlier on, but kept on getting an engaged signal. Why the devil didn't you ring, Elinor?"

"Oh, it's you, Miles."

"Is that relief I hear, or disappointment?"

"Relief," she said shakily. "I did ring you. You weren't there. I wasn't going to worry you, but I had someone playing games on the phone earlier."

"And you didn't let me know?" said Miles furiously. "Elinor, I've had enough of this. You're coming back here now!"

"I am not," she said indignantly. "The calls are a coincidence, probably nothing to do with you—"

She let out a sudden screech of fright as the house was suddenly plunged into darkness....

Dear Reader,

Welcome to the latest book in our HOLDING OUT
FOR A HERO series. Every month for a whole year
we'll be bringing you some of the world's most eligible
bachelors. They're handsome, they're charming, but,
best of all, they're single! And, as twelve lucky women
are about to discover, it's not finding Mr. Right that's
the problem—it's holding on to him!

This month it's the turn of acclaimed author
Catherine George, with her exciting story,
Fallen Hero (#3396). As a teenager, Elinor had
worshiped Miles Carew from afar. He was a man
worth waiting for! Now he was back! But it seemed
her hero was slightly tarnished—Miles had given
up on love. All he wanted was someone to help him
raise his daughter! And though Sophie was adorable,
Elinor wanted to be so much more to him than a
ready-made mom!

Look out next month for another book in our
exciting series, this time by award-winning author
Leigh Michaels. Karr Elliot is *The Only Man for Maggie*,
of that she's sure. All she needs to do is convince him
of the fact!

With best wishes,

The Editors

Harlequin Romance

Some men are worth waiting for!

Fallen Hero
Catherine George

Harlequin Books

TORONTO • NEW YORK • LONDON
AMSTERDAM • PARIS • SYDNEY • HAMBURG
STOCKHOLM • ATHENS • TOKYO • MILAN
MADRID • WARSAW • BUDAPEST • AUCKLAND

ISBN 0-373-03396-6

FALLEN HERO

First North American Publication 1996.

CHAPTER ONE

A MILE from home it began to snow. The small, solitary figure trudged on, angry with the elements which had turned so suddenly against her. The street-lights on this stretch of road were few and far between, and only made the darkness more intense once she left each radius of orange light behind.

Furious with herself for forgetting to book a taxi before she took the train from Cheltenham, Elinor had stormed along at first from the town. But now she was on the lonelier section of road she was slowing down, just when she could have done with some speed. Her overnight bag was beginning to feel like a ton weight and the strap of her overloaded handbag cut deep into one sodden shoulder. And to her dismay she was nervous. She knew every twist and turn of the road like the back of her hand, but in darkness, with a blizzard blowing up, it was lonely and deserted. The few houses she passed were long distances apart, most of them not even visible from the road.

Unexpectedly she felt vulnerable in the snow and dark here in the country. In Cheltenham there were shops and buildings and light, and a taxi always at hand. Here the hedges and trees rustled menacingly in the rising wind, which whipped strands of hair from her scarlet wool beret and stuck feathers of snow to her lashes. Her raincoat, perfectly adequate in the town, was useless on a country road with nowhere to shelter. Elinor shivered as her flat leather pumps

squelched along through snow beginning to coat the
road surface at alarming speed. Her impulse to come
home for the weekend had seemed such a brilliant,
obvious idea after the break with Oliver. Now she was
beginning to regret it.

Elinor Gibson had been born in Stavely, a village
tucked away in the triangle of Gloucestershire
bounded by two rivers, the Wye and the Severn. Her
parents, both doctors, had recently retired, and to
celebrate had gone on holiday to Australia to visit
relatives. Elinor had sped them happily on their way
a month before, never dreaming that a few weeks later
her life would have taken a turn in an entirely different direction. That particular news, she thought,
depressed, could keep until they got back. No point
in spoiling the holiday they'd looked forward to for
so long—even less in harbouring regrets of her own.

With a sigh of relief she saw the gates of Cliff House
come into view and quickened her pace past its stone
boundary walls. They lined the road for some distance, but just beyond lay her own home, and, gasping
with effort, she hurried as fast as she could past the
second entrance to Cliff House and turned up the
narrow drive to the large, rambling cottage where
she'd been born.

The house was in darkness, as she'd known it would
be. Breathing heavily, she dumped her bag down near
the front doorstep, tugged a wet woollen glove off
with her teeth and rummaged in her bag in the
darkness for her keys. Suddenly she let out a groan
of despair. Before making her dash for home she'd
been dressed ready for a party. The keys were probably
in the small suede bag on her dressing-table, where
they were precious little use to anybody.

She set out on a frantic tour of inspection, but Cliff Cottage had windows reinforced with secondary double glazing, and the outer stable-door at the front was not only inches thick and built of solid oak but opened into a porch guarded by an inner door made of toughened glass. At the back of the house there was another oak door, bolted and barred, as Elinor knew only too well, and every window in the place would have its security lock firmly in place.

She forced herself to calm down and think logically. There was no way she could break in. And at this hour she had no taste for knocking up one of the neighbours to beg a bed for the night, either. She leaned wearily on the kitchen window-ledge as she pictured the familiar comforts within, then an abrupt, unthinkable nightmare overtook her as her arms were caught behind her and a knife-point pricked her throat.

'Move, or make a sound, and you're dead!' breathed a voice in her ear.

The instruction was quite unnecessary. Elinor, dumb with terror, couldn't have uttered a word to save her life.

'Right, let's have a look at you,' said the deadly whisper.

Her arms were twisted to breaking-point as the knife was replaced by a torch which shone in her stunned eyes.

'What the——?' Her captor swore volubly as he let her go. 'Elinor Gibson? Why in hell's name are you creeping round at this time of night in the dark?' He shone the torch briefly on his hooded face to identify himself.

'Miles?' she croaked, shaking from rage now instead of terror. 'Miles Carew? *You* were the one creeping around, not me. What on earth were you playing at?'

'I promised your father I'd keep an eye on things,' he said brusquely. 'You're not supposed to be here.'

'It *is* my home,' she pointed out furiously, forgetting all her past awe of Miles Carew. 'I came away in a hurry and forgot my keys, that's all. And,' she added, with sudden vehemence, 'I would have had to wait ages for a taxi, so I've walked all the way from the station; I'm cold and wet, and the last thing I needed was all that macho nonsense just now!'

'Sorry I frightened you,' he said tersely, sounding anything but. 'I couldn't take any chances; there's a rash of break-ins in the neighbourhood.' He caught her by the arm. 'Come on, I'll take you up to the house to get dry while we think of some way of getting you in the cottage.'

'I wouldn't dream of troubling you——' she began haughtily, then bit her lip as she realised there was precious little alternative.

'Don't be silly,' he said wearily. 'Any luggage?'

'Behind the laurels near the front door.'

With the torch to guide them through the now blinding snow, Miles marched Elinor back down to the gate and turned up into the steep, winding drive to Cliff House, where a battery of security beams came on through the whirling flakes, lighting their way round the back of the house and into a blessedly warm, stone-flagged room which housed a washing-machine and drier and a pair of large refrigerators.

Miles slid back his hood as he stamped his boots free of snow, eyeing Elinor in amusement. She scowled, aware that her hair hung in rats' tails from the sodden red mass that had once been her beret, and that her nose was probably a matching shade of scarlet.

'You look terrible,' he commented as he hung his parka on a peg. 'Let me take your coat.'

Elinor plucked off her gloves and beret and undid her raincoat with stiff, cold fingers, wishing bitterly that she'd never left Cheltenham.

'You're probably wet through,' said Miles, hanging the coat on a peg. 'In which case a hot bath and a change of clothes are first on the agenda. Come straight upstairs. I'll bring your bag.'

Elinor trudged obediently through the large kitchen and up the stairs after her host, feeling hideously embarrassed. She would have liked to protest, but couldn't quite manage it. For one thing the suggestion was perfectly sensible, not to mention tempting, and for another Major Miles Carew of the Royal Green Jackets was very obviously used to having his orders obeyed at the double.

He ushered her into a bathroom she remembered very well, dumped her bag down and told her to get a move on.

Elinor ran hot water into the plain white tub, got into it with a sigh of relief, but didn't dare linger, much as she longed to. She soaped herself all over, used a loofah to get her circulation back to normal, then dried herself rapidly, wondering what Miles was doing here at Cliff House. If she'd had any idea he was in residence next door she might have thought twice about rushing back to Cliff Cottage. But probably not. After the row with Oliver she'd taken off for Stavely like a homing pigeon.

She towelled her thick hair as dry as possible, dressed swiftly in fresh underwear and a yellow wool shirt and black leggings, added a heavy black sweater on top and pulled on thick black wool socks and the rather scruffy flat black suede loafers she used for slippers. She rummaged in her handbag for a tortoiseshell clasp and caught back her wet hair, then picked up her overnight bag and went downstairs just as Miles emerged from the kitchen, tray in hand.

'Good,' he said approvingly as he caught sight of her. 'I was just coming to give you a shout.'

Elinor felt colour rise in her newly scrubbed face. 'I'm sorry to be such a nuisance.'

'Don't be silly. Go along and open the study door.'

She obeyed, feeling awkward as Miles brushed past to lay the tray down on a small table between a studded leather armchair and another covered in faded chintz. Logs crackled invitingly in the cowled fireplace, heavy damask curtains hid the howling blizzard outside from view, and suddenly she felt better.

It was years since Elinor had last been in the room, but nothing had changed. The deep, comfortable sofa stood in precisely the same place in front of the fire, the leather-topped table in the corner was still littered with papers and folders, with the same green-shaded brass lamp at one end. And the floor-to-ceiling bookshelves were crammed full of volumes of every description and taste, just as she remembered. The television in the corner was bigger and newer, and the video recorder beneath it was a new addition, but otherwise the room was comfortingly familiar.

The actual difference was her companion. When Elinor had come to Cliff House in the past it was always with Mark or Harry, or both. As a child she'd had the time of her life with the younger Carew boys in the wild, glorious gardens of Cliff House. By that stage their mother had been an invalid and their father always busy with his law practice. It had fallen to Mrs Hedley, their housekeeper, to dole out drinks and cakes and good-natured scoldings.

Miles, senior to his brothers by a great gulf of twelve years, had been a very superior being, away at school, then Oxford, Sandhurst, and on to his regiment. Elinor had seen him from time to time, secretly nourished an intense, teenage passion for the demi-god with the dark, saturnine good looks and the smart uniform, but until tonight she had never been in his company for any length of time. And now the drama of their encounter had dissipated a little she felt ir-ritatingly shy.

She sat down in the chintz-covered chair, eyeing the soup he gave her.

'Vegetable,' he informed her, sinking into the leather chair. 'It won't hurt you.'

She sighed despairingly. 'I'm terribly sorry, but it will. I'm allergic to onions.'

He stared at her for a moment, then took the bowl from her and put it back on the tray. 'How about tea?'

She nodded, flushing. 'I'd love some.'

'Right.' He got up. 'You pour the tea, I'll remove the soup and get myself a drink.'

Elinor poured tea from a silver pot into a thin flowered cup and wished, not for the first time that night, that she'd stayed sensibly in Cheltenham, braved the party without Oliver, or gone to bed with a book instead of running home without her keys. What an idiot! And what on earth was she going to do now? The moment she'd told her flatmate she was off to Stavely for a few days Linda had promptly invited her latest boyfriend to stay at the flat while Elinor was away. Playing gooseberry to a pair in the first throes of a love-affair was the last thing she wanted.

'That's a very black frown,' observed Miles, coming in with a plate of sandwiches. 'Don't worry, Elinor. You can stay here the night if that's the problem.' He put the sandwiches down beside her and handed her a plate. 'No onions, just ham. I hope you're not vegetarian?'

'No, I'm not.' She gave him a small, polite smile. 'Thank you. But you shouldn't have troubled.'

'If you've hiked all the way from Chepstow in this weather you're in need of something,' he said firmly, and stood with his back to the flames, watching as she began to eat. 'A pretty mad thing to do on your own at this time of night, by the way—anything could have happened.'

'The only harm I came to was a run-in with your horrible knife. I thought my time had come.' She glared at him, shyness forgotten. 'Did you have to be so melodramatic?'

He shrugged, his lean face inscrutable. 'I thought you were a burglar.'

'Would you really have used the knife?'

'The threat is usually enough.'

'You mean you've had intruders here before?' she said, alarmed.

'I was talking professionally,' he said without drama. 'Have some more tea.'

Elinor eyed him thoughtfully. Miles Carew was even more attractive than her youthful picture of him. His clothes were unremarkable enough—old desert boots, heavy cords and a tabbed khaki sweater worn over a wool shirt—but the tall body inside the clothes was slim and muscular, well-disciplined, like the lean-featured face. He had the rather swarthy skin typical of all the Carews, but in contrast to the wide clear grey of his siblings' eyes his were long and narrow, and, like his hair, the exact colour and gleam of expensive bitter chocolate.

'What's the matter?' he asked. 'You're eyeing me as though you've never seen me before.'

'I haven't often, and rarely at such close quarters,' she said candidly. 'I'm sorry. I didn't realise I was staring. I was just wondering what I'm going to do tonight.'

'That's obvious,' he said briskly, sitting down in the leather chair. 'It's past midnight—too late for a hotel or knocking up a neighbour. You'll stay here.'

Not, Would you like to stay here? thought Elinor wryly.

'Are you sure that's convenient?' she asked.

He frowned. 'Convenient? Why not? There are five bedrooms up there besides mine. Choose any one you like——' He smiled in sudden comprehension. 'Ah! You mean my bedroom might already have an occupant waiting for me to join her. Fear not, Elinor. There's no one here but you and me. The Hedleys are away.'

She looked at him for a moment, then nodded. 'You're very kind. Thank you. Have one of these.' She waved at the plate of sandwiches and Miles took one.

'I don't honestly think there's a way of getting into Cliff Cottage without some kind of damage,' he said eventually, finishing the sandwich. 'If the weather's not too bad I strongly advise a return to Cheltenham tomorrow.'

Elinor shook her head decisively. 'In the morning I'll ring Mrs Crouch. She gives mother a hand with the house. She might have a key.'

Miles plainly disapproved of the idea. 'Why are you so determined to spend time on your own here in this weather?'

'Are you trying to get rid of me, Miles?' she countered, without answering his question. 'I promise that once I'm in Cliff Cottage I won't bother you again.'

'You'll bother me a lot if you insist on staying there alone.'

'But why? Loads of people live alone round here, most of them women, too.'

Miles looked grim. 'They don't live over the wall from me.'

Something in his tone sent a cold shiver down Elinor's spine. 'Have you had any trouble here, then?'

'Yes.' He gave her a direct look. 'Haven't you noticed anything missing?'

'I'm not likely to—I don't know the house well enough,' she said, surprised.

'I meant the dog.'

Elinor's eyes widened as she thought of the Irish wolfhound taken care of by Tom Hedley, who looked after the Cliff House gardens. 'Of course! Normally she'd have been barking her head off...' She paused. 'What happened?'

'Yesterday someone threw poisoned meat over the hedge on the main drive. Fortunately Tom Hedley was out early and found it before I let Meg out. I've sent her off to kennels for the time being, as a safety precaution,' added Miles grimly.

Elinor went cold. 'How horrible! Who on earth would do something like that?'

'Someone bent on a war of nerves, I fancy. For myself I couldn't care less, but I can't risk danger to anyone else, so I sent the Hedleys on holiday until further notice. I'll stay on here alone until I find out whether someone intends trying something similar on me.'

'Don't even think about it!' Elinor shuddered, then looked at him questioningly. 'Are you on leave, then?'

'No. I retired from the army a little while ago.'

'Oh—I didn't know.' Elinor smiled awkwardly. 'I'm surprised. The boys used to say you'd end up as a general at the very least.'

'After the Gulf War I began to think of packing it in. I sent in my resignation once my thirty-seventh birthday qualified me for a pension. My wife, of course, had resigned from her role as Mrs Carew long before that.' Miles stared into the fire for a while, then turned to look at her. 'I assume you knew I was divorced?'

'Yes,' admitted Elinor. 'My mother told me. I— I'm sorry.'

Miles shrugged. 'It was on the cards right from the beginning. Selina always hated army life, couldn't take the *roulement* periods when I went off with my unit to Belize or Cyprus without her. She's an actress with a career of her own, so not unnaturally she made a life for herself while I was away. Eventually there was no place in it for me.'

Elinor sat very still, hardly able to believe she was here in Cliff House, privy to confidences from its

owner. Miles Carew had always been such a distant
figure, so different from Harry and Mark that she'd
always been in awe of him.

'I must be boring you,' he said, suddenly brisk, as
he got to his feet. 'I'll show you where you can sleep.'

Elinor waited a moment before getting to her feet.
'How about Sophie? Do you see her often?' For a
moment she held her breath, fully expecting a snub,
but Miles's hard face softened.

'Sophie's been convalescing from chicken-pox with
me. The Hedleys spoil my daughter outrageously,
needless to say. But after the incident with the
poisoned meat I packed her off to Shropshire immediately with the Hedleys. Mrs Hedley's sister runs
a small private hotel near Ludlow. I couldn't send
Sophie back to her mother. Selina's in the Caribbean
with my successor,' he added without inflexion.

'Do you know who tried to poison the poor dog?'
asked Elinor rather hastily.

'No. But in the course of my career I've trodden
on the toes of various nationalities and religious be-
liefs. It could be anyone.' He smiled bleakly. 'I was
rather disappointed when my intruder turned out to
be the girl next door, Elinor. I'd hoped to catch
whoever it is and get on with my life.'

'What if your quarry catches you first?'

He shrugged. 'Then my worries will be over
anyway.'

Elinor got up, pulling a face. 'I feel I ought to
apologise for being me.'

Miles looked at her at length, as though he was
seeing her clearly for the first time. 'You don't seem
to have grown much since the days you were running

wild with the boys. But your hair's different. It used to be fair.'

'It still is. It's just wet.'

Miles frowned as he touched her head to see for himself. 'Hell, you'll catch cold if you go to bed like that. There's an old hairdrier around somewhere. I'll hunt it out.'

'Thank you.' She smiled diffidently. 'I stayed here once when I was little. My parents were away at a conference and your mother offered to have me until they got back. I slept in the little room at the back, at the end of the upstairs hall. It had flowery wallpaper. I loved it.'

'Good, because that's where I've put you tonight— mainly because it's the room Sophie was using and the bed's aired. You'll have to put up with her bedclothes, I'm afraid, but the room's the warmest in the house so you should be comfortable enough.'

'It beats camping out in the back garden of Cliff Cottage,' said Elinor drily.

She followed him upstairs, past a row of closed doors in the upper hall to the small room at the end, which, unlike most of the others had an adjoining bathroom all to itself. Her bag had been placed at the end of the bed, which seemed to have the same flowered quilt she remembered of old.

She eyed the battered teddy on the bed with misgiving. 'Oh, dear—did Sophie forget him?'

'No. He lives here.' Miles looked oddly embarrassed. 'Actually he was mine, back in the mists of time. Sophie likes him to sleep with her when she visits.'

'Thank goodness!' Elinor smiled. 'I had visions of Mrs Hedley trying to soothe an inconsolable Sophie at bedtime.'

Miles stared bleakly at the bear. 'I hope not. She objected strongly to the transfer to Ludlow. But under the circumstances I couldn't risk having her here until I clear this business up.'

'You miss her already,' said Elinor with sympathy.

He nodded. 'I've got used to having her around. She's with me permanently now, by the way. Selina's marrying again, and the new man doesn't fancy a six-year-old stepdaughter as part of the package.'

'How does Sophie feel about the new arrangement?'

'Thrilled to bits—and so am I.' Miles grinned, looking suddenly younger.

Elinor laughed. 'I hope you know what you're taking on!'

'Sophie's had a raw deal lately. Since Selina got a plum role in a new drama series she's had no time for her child. Sophie goes to school in the day, of course, but afterwards a nanny looks after her. Nice woman, but too staid for a tomboy like Sophie. She's the same sort of child you were—hair always untidy and mud on her clothes.'

'Thanks!'

He grinned. 'At first sight tonight you hadn't changed much either. You looked like a drowned rat!'

'You said something about a hairdrier,' Elinor reminded him tartly.

It took Miles some time to hunt one down. When he returned Elinor was still fully dressed, but she'd brushed her teeth and slapped cream on to a face which felt raw after its run-in with the elements. When the tap sounded on the door she opened it, took the hairdrier, and thanked her host once more.

'Not at all,' he said briskly. 'I'm only too glad I found you tonight.'

Elinor frowned. 'Which reminds me, why were you outside so late in this weather?'

'I got out on patrol at regular intervals,' he said casually. 'When I got near the fence I heard a noise next door at the cottage and came to investigate. You know the rest.'

'Would you really have used a knife if it had been an intruder?' she asked curiously.

'Not unless obliged to, and then only as persuasion.' His smile turned her blood cold.

She looked at him thoughtfully. 'It's none of my business, I know, but this is no ordinary burglar by the sound of it—not if he tried to kill Meg.'

'On the contrary, professional burglars can be surprisingly ruthless.' Miles paused. 'And in the circumstances, Elinor, I really would be happier if you caught a train back to Cheltenham tomorrow.'

'There's no danger to me, Miles, and if Mrs Crouch has a key I really do want to stay for a few days.' She smiled a little, and explained why returning to her flat would be embarrassing for the time being. 'So, if you'll just let me phone Mrs C in the morning, I'll move into Cliff Cottage and lock myself in—you won't know I'm there.'

Miles looked down at her for a moment, then shrugged. 'I can't order you back, I know——'

'That's right, Major,' she agreed sweetly.

'It's plain mister from now on,' he reminded her, and smiled. 'Not to you, of course, Little Nell. You were a surprise in more ways than one tonight. Somehow I hadn't realised you'd grown up.'

'Same age as Harry, remember?' she returned lightly. 'Twenty-five last month. I saw him the other day, incidentally. He's joined the family law firm, he told me. Odd to think of Harry as a solicitor, somehow. I always thought he'd join the army like you and Mark.'

'My father would have liked us all in the firm, carrying on family tradition,' said Miles wryly. 'At least one of us hasn't disappointed him.'

'*You* can't have,' said Elinor, surprised. 'Not with your service career—getting promoted so early, not to mention the decoration. When the Gulf War was on I used to sit glued to the television news every night to see if you were on TV. Then Harry told me you were involved in pretty hush-hush sort of stuff and your face would never appear on screen any-way——'

'Harry talks too much,' said Miles quickly. 'Now dry that hair and get some sleep, Elinor. Goodnight.'

Elinor sat for some time with the drier until the heavy layers of hair were back to their usual colour scheme of every shade from beige to ash-blonde. When she was a child her mother had despaired of trying to keep the thick mane tidy and kept it short like a boy's, so that when Elinor played with Harry and Mark it had been hard to distinguish one from the other. Now the hair fell gleaming to her shoulders, and no one could mistake Elinor Gibson for anything other than a small, curvaceous specimen of the female sex.

CHAPTER TWO

THE bed in Sophie's room was wonderfully warm and comfortable and Elinor felt very tired. But she slept fitfully, sure at intervals that even through the re-inforced glass of the windows she could hear noises outside above the howling wind.

At one stage she woke to find the room lit up like day as all the outside security lights came blazing on. Sitting bolt upright, heart thumping, she took some time to persuade herself that the culprit was a badger or a fox. Miles was a long way away in what had for-merly been his parents' room, right at the other end of the house, and Elinor couldn't forget that at least three of the bedrooms at the front of the house had a balcony running the length of them—a balcony all too easy to climb. The boys had shared one of the big front bedrooms in the old days, and in summer it had always been far more fun to shin up the balcony to climb in through the window rather than use the stairs.

First light came earlier than usual for a February morning, courtesy of the snow's reflection on the bedroom ceiling. Elinor jumped out of bed to draw the curtains and peer out. The window looked down on the Wye, almost three hundred feet below, but today the view was veiled by a fluttering curtain of wind-blown white flakes, and the garden hid under a thick blanket of snow.

At this rate, she thought, shivering, she wouldn't be going anywhere, Cheltenham included. And surely any self-respecting intruder would abandon his plans in this weather?

Elinor dressed quickly in the clothes of the night before, this time adding a pair of thick black tights. Cliff House, despite its central heating, was large and draughty and obviously took a while to warm up in the morning.

There wasn't a sound in the house as she ventured along the upper hall. Hoping Miles wouldn't object if she went down to the kitchen and made a hot drink, she stole past the end wing where he slept and went downstairs, only to find him already seated at the breakfast-table in the vast kitchen, and the air full of mouth-watering scents of bacon and toast and coffee.

'Good morning,' she said, smiling shyly. 'It was so quiet I thought you might still be asleep.'

'I wake early—old habits die hard.' He jumped up to hold out a chair for her. 'Coffee and toast already available, but what else would you like? Bacon? Eggs?'

Elinor shook her head quickly. 'No, thanks. Toast will be fine.'

Miles returned to his chair, looking at her with such concentration that Elinor frowned as she poured herself some coffee.

'What is it?'

'You look different this morning.'

'Surprising what a spot of make-up and dry hair will do for a girl,' she responded cheerfully.

Miles smiled in agreement. 'I'd forgotten that variegated hair of yours. Are those streaks still natural?'

Elinor nodded. 'I'm always meaning to turn a hairdresser loose on it to get it more uniform.'

'Absolutely not! Leave it as it is.' He smiled and pushed the toast-rack towards her. 'Did you sleep well?'

'The bed was so comfortable I should have done.' She smiled ruefully. 'To be honest I kept imagining noises outside. When the lights went on I was convinced your intruder was on the move again.'

He nodded. 'I had a quick look round but nothing was visible through the snow. Probably some member of the animal world on the prowl.'

'I told myself that but I didn't convince me!'

'If I'd known you were awake I'd have come along to report.' One of his slim dark brows rose. 'Are you still determined to stay on?'

'Yes—if Mrs Crouch has a key.'

'And if she doesn't?'

Elinor met his eyes very directly. 'I'll nip back on the train and collect mine.'

Miles drank his coffee, eyeing her thoughtfully. 'You're very determined about this. With your parents away I would have thought you'd be glad to stay in Cheltenham. What brought you back to Cliff Cottage?'

Elinor kept her eyes on the toast she was buttering. 'I've just come adrift from the man I've...been seeing for the past year.'

'Was the agreement to part mutual?'

'No, it wasn't. The breaking-up process was very hard to take, as a matter of fact. I suddenly felt desperate to get away.'

Miles leaned over to refill her coffee-cup. 'Poor little Nell——'

'I wish you wouldn't call me that,' she snapped. 'I'm no Dickens fan, nor am I all that little any more. Harry and Mark call me that at their peril these days.'

'Then I won't either,' he said promptly, lips twitching. 'Though you *are* small, Elinor. Perfectly formed, I might add, but definitely small!'

She smiled unwillingly, and he nodded in approval.

'That's better. This man of yours,' he added, 'did he take off with another woman?'

'No.' Elinor drew designs on the tablecloth with the tip of her spoon. 'I was the one who took off.' She sighed, depressed. 'There were scenes.'

'I see. You came home to escape recriminations.'

'Afraid so. I hated upsetting Oliver. He's a nice man. But I couldn't go on pretending.'

'"Nice"?' repeated Miles, raising a slim dark eyebrow. 'Poor bloke. I hope no one ever refers to me as "nice".'

'Don't worry, Miles,' she retorted, chuckling, 'I doubt anyone will, somehow.'

'I'm relieved. So did nice Oliver want to be your friend, lover or husband?'

'All three. He achieved the first two, but lately he's been talking weddings and dates and, well, I found I rebelled at the thought of it.' She bit her lip. 'He was pretty bitter about it, said I misled him, that when we became lovers he assumed marriage was a foregone conclusion.' She flushed a little. 'And I really thought so too, at the time. I mean, I wouldn't have—have got in so deep otherwise. But I spent part of Christmas with Oliver and his family, and he's taken me home for Sunday lunch occasionally since. Last Sunday I suddenly got horribly claustrophobic. I mutinied at the thought of doing the same thing at intervals for the foreseeable future.'

'Then you did the right thing to cut loose,' Miles said with decision. 'Marriage is tricky enough when you both start off convinced it's happy-ever-after time.'

'Is that how it was for you?' asked Elinor diffidently.

'Oh, yes. Very much so.' His smile was sardonic. 'I met Selina when I was at Sandhurst and still wet behind the ears. We got engaged at the passing-out ball—every glittering, romantic cliché in the book. And still it didn't work out. We were far too young to tie ourselves up, as it turned out, because we matured in very different ways. My life was the army, Selina's the stage. At first, at least—she sticks to television these days. And she's marrying a very wealthy man this time, so maybe her second crack at marriage will be more successful than the first with me.'

Once more Elinor was struck by the strangeness of being alone with Miles Carew, breakfasting with him, telling him things about Oliver she hadn't yet discussed with a soul.

'Why the pensive look?' he asked.

'I was just thinking how odd and—and yet how comfortable it is to be here with you like this. I've always been scared to death of you before.'

'Scared?' he said, astounded. 'Why?'

Elinor shrugged. 'Harry and Mark were very much in awe of you when we were children, so naturally enough I was too. I was thirteen—and very impressionable—when you married Selina. I thought it was just a fairy-tale when Mother and Dad came home from the wedding to tell me about it: the guard of honour with swords, and Selina so beautiful in her white dress and you in your uniform.'

Miles smiled derisively. 'The fairy-tale ground to a halt fairly quickly. And Sophie's unplanned arrival made things worse instead of better. Selina wasn't happy about motherhood.' He gave Elinor an odd, almost embarrassed look. 'Sorry. You must be very easy to talk to. Normally I don't discuss my marriage with anyone.'

'I haven't told anyone about Oliver, either.'

To break an odd little silence Elinor rose to her feet in a hurry.

'Could I ring Mrs Crouch now, please?'

'Of course. If your mind is made up——'

'It is!'

'There's a phone in the hall, another in the study. Take your pick.' Miles opened the kitchen door for her. 'Where does Mrs Crouch live?'

'About a mile down Springfield Lane.' Elinor smiled. 'Thank you for breakfast.'

Mrs Crouch was indeed at home, and surprised that Elinor thought she could have been anywhere else in such weather. To Elinor's delight she admitted to having a key to Cliff Cottage in her possession.

'Only mind you bring it back when you go, Elinor,' she warned, 'or I won't be able to keep things nice up there for your mother.'

'I won't forget. And I'll be very tidy, I promise.'

'That'll be the day,' retorted Mrs Crouch.

Elinor went back to the kitchen.

'All set,' she said briskly. 'Mrs C does have a key so I'll be on my way.'

'You can't walk down there in this. I'll get the Range Rover out,' said Miles firmly. 'And I shall expect a phone call at regular intervals once you're installed in the cottage.'

Elinor eyed him closely. 'I wish you'd tell me who—or what—you're expecting, Miles.'

He shrugged. 'I don't know. But I'm going to find out. In the meantime I'll just take every precaution. Your arrival was a factor I didn't bargain for.'

'You mustn't worry about me, Miles—I'll be fine. Mother's freezer will be packed with food, and I've got a couple of videos and three novels in my bag——'

'No wonder it's so heavy! I'll drive you down, see you into the house, get the heating going and then bring you back up here to collect your things and have some lunch,' he said decisively.

Elinor gave him a wry smile. 'Yes, sir, Major, sir!'

'Enough of that,' he advised, unmoved, and handed her an elderly waxed jacket. 'Your raincoat's still sodden. Wear this old thing of Harry's.'

Miles turned up the sleeves on the jacket and fastened it as though she were Sophie, then handed her a shapeless tweed hat.

'Harry's fishing hat,' he said, grinning at her when she'd put it on. 'Not glamorous, but better than getting your hair wet again. Come on, let's sprint for the coach-house.'

Half an hour later they were back at Cliff Cottage, where Miles made Elinor stay outside until he'd searched the house.

'But if I couldn't get in how could anyone else manage it?' she demanded impatiently when she was finally admitted.

'If someone wants to get in they will,' Miles informed her. 'It's unlikely here, because your father installed a burglar alarm and had the windows reinforced, but it's best to make sure.'

'You're making me nervous,' she said irritably as they went through to the kitchen.

'Good. If you're nervous you'll be vigilant,' he said coolly. 'I'll re-programme the boiler.'

Once the heating was going and a few lamps were switched on Miles took Elinor back to Cliff House for lunch.

'By this afternoon your place will be warm, and I'll know you've had at least one good meal today,' he said as they battled their way through the wind. 'Good. The snow's stopped.'

'Thanks heavens for that,' gasped Elinor, grabbing at the ridiculous hat. 'Golly, what weather—it's too late in the year for all this snow!'

When they got in the house Elinor made a beeline for the kettle, while Miles went off to ring Mrs Hedley and have a chat with his daughter. When he returned to the kitchen he was grinning.

'Sophie's graciously consented to forgive me. Mrs Hedley's sister owns a labrador bitch by the name of Daisy, and Daisy, bless her, has recently produced six puppies. As far as I can gather Sophie spends every waking minute helping Daisy bring up her babies.'

Elinor laughed as she poured coffee. 'I hope Daisy's suitably grateful!'

'If Daisy isn't, I am,' said Miles, suddenly sober. 'Sophie couldn't see why Meg had to go off to kennels, even less why she herself was packed off with Hedleys. Daisy is providing her with good therapy for her indignation.'

'A lot better than knowing the truth,' said Elinor with a shiver, then became purposely brisk. 'If you'll tell me what you had in mind for lunch I could get on with it.'

Miles produced a tin of lobster bisque, the remains of a large ham and the ingredients for a mixed salad.

'Mrs Hedley left me a few things in the freezer, but I can't guarantee a lack of onions,' he said as he operated a tin-opener deftly, 'so a cold meal is the best I can do.'

'Exactly the type of thing I enjoy most,' Elinor assured him. She put together a salad, concocted a dressing to toss it in, cut thick slices from one of Mrs Hedley's home-made loaves, then laid the large oak table while Miles heated soup and carved the ham.

'What a team,' he said triumphantly as they sat down to steaming bowls of soup. 'If I'd known I was to have a visitor I'd have asked Mrs Hedley to leave a pudding of some kind. I'm not fond of sweet things myself, but there must be ice-cream in the freezer. Sophie adores the stuff.'

'Not for me,' Elinor said firmly. 'I put on weight if I even look at anything sweet. A little abstinence will do me good.'

'Does this Oliver of yours know where you are, by the way?'

'I didn't tell him I was coming home, no. In fact I told Linda to keep it to herself. She and Oliver aren't exactly soul mates, so she won't tell him a thing. Not,' she added, 'that he's likely to ask. He washed his hands of me in the end, once I'd convinced him it was over.'

'He's probably calmed down by now.'

'I doubt it.' She pulled a face. 'I hurt his vanity, as well as his feelings.'

'Few men relish being dumped,' said Miles shortly.

Elinor looked up at him in surprise. 'Surely that isn't how you see your own situation? Besides, Selina dumped the army rather than you, from what you've told me.'

He smiled sardonically. 'How good you are for my ego, Elinor. But the unvarnished truth is that while I was away, serving Queen and country, Selina found someone else. Someone, as she explained, who would be around constantly instead of swanning off to play war-games for months at a time, and, best of all, had the money to support her in luxury whether she worked or not.' He shrugged. 'Selina's astute. She knows her particular type of career depends on her face and figure. She's no character actress. When her looks go she'll fade gracefully into a retirement cushioned by the wealth of Lloyd Forbes—he of the pharmaceutical empire.'

'Oh, I see.' Elinor helped herself to salad. 'Do you still mind?'

'If I do it's solely because the divorce made Sophie desperately insecure. I'm determined to remedy that by providing a stable lifestyle here in Stavely with me— and by sending her to the village school rather than off to boarding-school next year, as Selina planned.'

'Boarding-school at seven!' said Elinor, horrified. 'Poor little mite.'

'Quite so,' said Miles grimly. 'I was thirteen before I went away, and believe me it was bad enough at that age. I shed quite a few secret tears at first.'

'Did you really?' Elinor smiled a little. 'I was just a baby then.'

He gave her an odd look. 'So you were.'

'The age-difference is negligible now,' she said hastily.

'I'm relieved! For a moment there I felt like Methuselah.'

Once the meal was over Elinor found she was reluctant to leave. She felt secure here in the big kitchen at Cliff House. With Miles. But when the meal was cleared away there was no excuse to linger, and with reiterated thanks she insisted on moving into the cottage before dark.

'Does that mean you're nervous?'

'Not exactly. But I'd like to get settled as soon as possible—see what food's on offer and so on.'

'If you're so hell-bent on staying in Stavely you'd do far better to stick to Cliff House,' he said, frowning.

Sorely tempted, she somehow found the strength to refuse. 'It's very kind of you, Miles, but no, thanks. I'll leave you in peace.'

The snow was beginning again as he took her back to Cliff Cottage. Once inside, he put her bag down in the hall and held out his hand.

'Goodbye for now, Elinor. Ring me. Promise?'

Elinor did so gladly, thanked him again rather formally for taking her in, then saw him out, locked both the outer and inner door, and went round the house, turning on lights against the gloom. In her small, cosy bedroom under the eaves the ceiling sloped down to a window with a deep, cushioned seat which had been the scene of many a daydream in Elinor's life in the past, quite a lot of which had featured Miles Carew.

She smiled wryly at the memory and, reassured by the familiarity of her surroundings, hung up what few clothes she'd brought, put two of her novels on the bedside table, then took the other book and the videos downstairs and went to investigate her mother's freezer. As expected it was crammed full of all kinds of delicacies. She would do very well for several days, if need be.

She put a carton of her mother's tomato and basil sauce in the microwave to defrost, then drew all the curtains and curled up on the sitting-room sofa with the novel she'd been looking forward to reading when she had time to herself. Now she had time to spare but found it unexpectedly hard to concentrate. She frowned, irritated with herself, and doggedly went on reading, but the telephone interrupted her before she was halfway through the first chapter of what promised to be a very gripping thriller. Expecting Linda or Miles, she answered with a friendly hello. But the only response was an odd silence, followed by a faint chuckle which raised the hairs on the back of her neck.

'Who is this?' she demanded angrily, but the line went dead and Elinor slammed down the phone, her hand shaking. First Miles with his cloak-and-dagger warnings and now some practical joker having fun! Furious because she was frightened, she went into the kitchen to make herself some coffee.

The phone rang twice more in the next few minutes, each time with the same silence on the line followed by the same chuckle.

After the third call Elinor felt well and truly spooked and rang Miles to report on the incidents, but there was no answer. Feeling utterly vulnerable, she left the receiver off the hook and went into the kitchen to cook tagliolini to eat with the tomato sauce.

With the radio on for company the humdrum familiarity of preparing a meal soothed her jagged nerves and she quickly felt calmer. She knew nuisance calls were common enough, but personal experience of them was unexpectedly terrifying. Especially in the present circumstances.

She ate her dinner from a tray in front of the television, then read for a while with the radio on low. At ten she felt she could decently go to bed, but found it took an enormous effort to switch off all the ground-floor lights. In the end she left one burning in the kitchen and another in the hall. If, heaven forbid, she had to come downstairs in the night, it would be easier with a light to give her courage.

She had a hot bath, then retired to bed to read. Once she settled in her own familiar bed it occurred to her that she'd never actually slept alone in the house before. It had seemed such a wonderful idea to escape here to Cliff Cottage after the confrontation with Oliver, but now she was *in situ* it didn't seem like a good idea at all. It was Miles's fault. Or the fault of the idiot waging a war of nerves against him. Which, of course, was the whole point. Whatever was happening was directed at Miles Carew, not Elinor Gibson!

Deeply relieved at the thought, she abandoned her book, went downstairs to put the phone back on the hook, then settled back down in the bed, leaving the radio playing and her bedside lamp on.

She was almost asleep when the phone rang again. She shot up in bed, heart thumping, hoping that whoever it was would give up and go away. But the ringing went on and on. In the end she tore out of bed and ran to the phone in her parents' room, snatching up the receiver, her voice hoarse and un-steady with fright as she answered.

'I expected a phone call to report all was well,' said Miles, sounding irritable. 'I rang several times earlier on, but kept getting an engaged signal. Why the devil didn't you ring, Elinor?'

She sat down suddenly on the edge of the bed. 'Oh, it's you, Miles.'

'Is that relief I hear, or disappointment?'

'Relief,' she said shakily. 'I did ring you earlier. You weren't there.'

'I must have been out on a recce. With the best part of four acres to patrol it takes a while.'

'I think you're mad to risk it.' She cleared her throat. 'I wasn't going to worry you, but I had someone playing games on the phone earlier.'

'And you didn't let me know?' said Miles furi-ously. 'Elinor, I've had enough of this. You're coming back here now!'

'I am not,' she said indignantly. 'The calls are a coincidence, probably nothing to do with you——' She let out a sudden screech of fright as the house was suddenly plunged into darkness.

'Elinor?' Miles bawled in her ear. 'What happened?'

'The electricity just went off,' she quavered, teeth chattering. 'Is yours still on?'

'Yes, it is! Now listen,' he ordered. 'Stay perfectly still. Don't move. I'll be down in two minutes. I'll hammer on the back door, three long, three short, so you'll know it's me.' He rang off, and Elinor pulled her mother's quilt round her shoulders and sat, heart thumping. The creaks and groans of an old house at night were magnified to a terrifying degree, convincing her that someone was trying to get in.

It seemed like a very long time before she saw a torch flash at the window and disappear round the back of the house. A moment later the promised knocks rapped on the door, loud and authoritative, three long and three short, repeated at regular intervals as she crept down the stairs in the dark, the kitchen floor like ice beneath her bare feet as she went to the back door.

'Elinor?' shouted Miles. 'For God's sake open the *door.*'

Clumsy with relief, she unlocked the door and shot back the bolts, and then Miles was inside the kitchen, slamming the bolts home before he said a word to her.

'I'll check the rest of the house—stay here,' he ordered.

'Not on your life! I'm coming with you.'

He went silently ahead of her through the ground-floor rooms, then up the stairs and on a swift, comprehensive search through the bedrooms. Once he was satisfied no one was there he pushed her into her own room and closed the door. Elinor sank down on the window-seat, feeling shattered.

'No time for that,' Miles said brusquely. He shone the torch around, then made for the dressing-table to light candles in small Victorian pottery holders. In the dim light he turned, looming tall in a bulky parka in the sloping-ceilinged room.

'I'll hold the torch while you pack a few necessities. The sooner you're out of here the better.'

'But——'

'No buts. Do as I say—at the double,' he added, in a tone which sent Elinor scurrying to stuff some belongings in the bag she'd only recently unpacked. She grabbed a candle and went into the bathroom to collect a few things and pull on her clothes, then went back to Miles, who was standing at her window, staring out into the night.

'The chuckle on the phone,' he said, turning. 'Was it male?'

'Yes. Soft and—and somehow hateful,' she said with a shiver.

'Then why the hell didn't you ring me again?'

Elinor turned away to rummage in her wardrobe for an old sheepskin jacket. 'I didn't want to be a nuisance,' she muttered.

'God grant me patience,' grated Miles, and snuffed out the candles before striding to the door. 'Now come on. *Move!*'

Elinor moved. She flew after Miles down the stairs and through the hall into the kitchen, flattening herself against the wall alongside him as he locked the back door, then took the hand he thrust out to haul her along at top speed beside him round the cottage and down the drive, then up the punishingly steep bends to the house, where the lights came on obligingly, lighting up the garden like a film set.

The feeling of relief once they were safe inside Cliff House was so intense that Elinor's knees shook as she took off her jacket in the old scullery, and stamped the snow from her ancient fur-lined boots. Miles thrust her into the kitchen and down into a chair at the table, then put a kettle on to boil before ringing the emergency service of the local electricity board. Afterwards he put the phone on the table and sat down beside her. He took her hand in his and held it firmly, as though to underline what he had to say.

'Elinor,' he said trenchantly, 'it's time you took all this seriously. You probably think I'm making a big drama out of nothing, but you're wrong. Drama isn't my scene. I've got a gut feeling that someone's out to damage me in some way. I don't mean murder. If it were I think the bastard would have got on with it by now. But you may as well know I've had phone calls myself—same as yours. I didn't want to frighten you, but I bloody well should have so you'd take notice.'

She stared at him, her eyes like saucers in a face suddenly paper-white. 'You think whoever it is has cut the electricity off at the cottage?'

'Yes. In a general power cut this house would be off too.' Miles released her hand and got up to make two mugs of coffee. 'Here,' he said, rejoining her. 'Drink this.'

Elinor sipped gratefully, then looked at him, puzzled. 'If this man wants to harass *you*, why would he start on me?'

'Because unless I'm very much mistaken,' he said, making it plain that he regarded this as virtually impossible, 'we're dealing with someone trained in the same line as me. He's probably been watching the house for days. I'm convinced he knows me—well enough to know that danger holds no fear for me personally. But where others are concerned I'm vulnerable.' His mouth tightened. 'I thought I'd removed my Achilles' heel by sending Sophie off with the Hedleys. Then you came on the scene.'

She bit her lip. 'And he's sure he'll upset you more by threatening Sophie or me rather than you yourself?'

His lips twitched. 'I don't think the word is "upset", precisely, but yes, that's the general gist. I was mad to let you move into the cottage today.'

Her chin lifted. 'What's all this about "letting" me, Miles? It was my choice. I refused to go back to Cheltenham, and I insisted on staying alone at the cottage against your wishes. The responsibility's mine, Major.'

'Not any more.' He drank down his coffee. 'Elinor, if I could I'd put you on a train back to Cheltenham right this minute, but the trains weren't running today anyway, so that isn't an option. But tomorrow I'll drive you back.'

'No, you won't,' she said indignantly.

'Yes, I will,' he retorted, 'even if I have to book you into a hotel.'

Elinor stared at him mutinously, then stiffened as the telephone rang. Miles looked at the light glowing on the mobile phone then, picking it up, barked a terse, 'Yes?' into it, listened for a moment, his mouth tightening, then pressed the off button and thrust down the aerial.

'Our friend,' he said grimly. He sat down beside Elinor, his eyes sardonic. 'By the look on your face I take it you're convinced.'

'Yes.' She gulped down the last of her coffee, then eyed him questioningly. 'Have you rung the police?'

He shook his head. 'That's the last resort. After all, what do I have to report? There's been no break-in, no damage to property. Our man made no actual threats on the phone, and the power cut at your place could be due to some ordinary fault, courtesy of the snow.' His face darkened. 'I'll deal with this myself.'

Elinor shivered. 'If it's a war of nerves it's a great success—with me, if not with you. I couldn't even switch the lights off to go to bed tonight.'

'Then why the blazes did you insist on going back there?'

'Pride!' She flashed him a defiant little smile. 'I wouldn't admit to being frightened. But to be honest it was a terrible effort to leave here after lunch.'

Miles glared at her for a moment, then his face softened. 'You always were a feisty little kid.'

'I'm amazed you ever noticed me!'

'Harry and Mark unfailingly got in hot water when you were around. If your school holidays didn't coincide with theirs things were noticeably quieter.'

'Ah! It was my absence you noticed, not me!'

He nodded morosely. 'I wish you were absent right now.'

Elinor scowled, but he took the wind out of her sails with the smile he employed so rarely.

'Only because I'm concerned for your safety, Elinor. Otherwise I could wish for nothing better than your company.'

'No need for the soft soap,' she said gruffly. 'Thank you for rescue mark two. I'd better take myself off to bed. I assume I'm in Sophie's room again?'

'No.' Miles held out his hand as he got to his feet. 'Tonight you share mine, Elinor.'

CHAPTER THREE

ELINOR stared at him, so astounded that Miles shook with sudden laughter.

'I'm glad you think it's so funny,' she said furiously.

He sobered quickly. 'Believe me, I don't, Elinor. There's nothing remotely funny about the whole situation. But with you at the other end of the house I can't guarantee your safety if our friend tries his hand at a spot of breaking and entering.' His eyes softened. 'Bed and board—even the odd spot of rescue—come free here, Little Nell. Besides, I don't look on you in that light——'

'Thanks!'

'I *mean*,' he went on patiently, 'that to me you're on a par with Sophie. Someone to protect, not—er—ravish.'

Oddly nettled, Elinor eyed him resentfully. 'You could have made that clear first.'

His mouth twisted. 'I'm just a straightforward soldier, remember, regrettably unversed in subtleties.'

'And I'm the Christmas fairy!'

They looked at each other in silence for a moment, then Miles's lips twitched. 'Perhaps I should have mentioned that my bedroom leads to a dressing-room, complete with single bed. You can sleep in there, safe from all comers. To get to you an intruder would have to get to me first. And there's no danger of that,' he added, with quiet conviction.

Elinor felt foolish. 'Sorry,' she muttered.

'What for?'

'For getting the wrong end of the stick—and, well, just for being here, giving you a whole load of trouble you could do without.'

Miles shrugged and lifted her bag. 'I won't pretend your presence isn't a responsibility, but it has its compensations. Barring Sophie's I've enjoyed precious little female company lately.'

Elinor eyed his straight back in surprise as she followed him up the stairs. 'No replacement for Selina in view, then?'

'No,' he said curtly, and opened the door into a bathroom at the head of the stairs. 'This was once another bedroom, which is why it opens on to the landing. Once we're settled for the night that door can be bolted, as you see, but I'll leave the connecting door into my bedroom open, in case you need a visit to the bathroom during the night.'

Hoping devoutly that that wouldn't be necessary, Elinor looked in admiration at the large bath in the centre of the room. The blue delft tiles surrounding it also bordered the small, white-painted fireplace, and there were leafy green plants on the divider which screened the lavatory enthroned in a corner of the room, more in front of the shower stall. And by day, she knew, the windows in two of the walls would give views of one of the horseshoe bends in the River Wye far below.

'It looks like a page out of a glossy magazine,' she said, to counter the hint of constraint in the air.

'I had it redesigned for Selina,' said Miles, shrugging. 'A wasted effort, as it turned out. She's never even seen it.'

Keeping her thoughts to herself, Elinor followed him through a large room furnished with a wide bed, a tall chest of drawers and a dressing-table with a triple mirror. The tobacco-brown of the velvet stool and small squabbed chair echoed the stripes of the heavy cream linen curtains, and the dark pine furniture was in the style popular in the early part of Victoria's reign, before opulence and ornate carving overtook Regency-style restraint.

Elinor looked round in admiration. 'Lovely room. So much space.'

'That's because my father dispensed with a pair of rather overpowering wardrobes and had some built in here instead.' He opened a door on the far side of the room and showed Elinor into a small apartment with two walls lined with floor-to-ceiling cupboards painted in white, a third wall lined with a mirror, a single bed covered with a double quilt below the window in the fourth. 'Will you be all right in here?'

Elinor smiled at him gratefully. 'Of course I will. It's good of you to go to all this trouble.'

Miles looked at her for a moment. 'I won't pretend I wouldn't prefer you safe and sound back in your own flat, Elinor. But since you are here in Stavely I'll sleep a damn sight more easily with you in here rather than on your own in the cottage.' He moved to the door. 'I'll go on my usual rounds for a few minutes, then I'll be back. By that time I expect to find you tucked up in bed, preferably asleep.'

Elinor saluted pertly. 'Yes sir, Major, sir!'

He grinned. 'Glad to see your sense of humour's still functioning.'

*　*　*

As she got ready for bed at top speed Elinor was rather surprised to find that Miles was right. Earlier on she'd found it impossible to find anything amusing about the entire situation, but here, safe and sound in a room guarded by Major Miles Carew, ex-SAS, she couldn't help smiling at the utter absurdity of it all. Oliver had been the only man she'd ever slept with up to now, and in retrospect it wasn't an experience she looked back on with undiluted pleasure. Yet tonight she had no qualms about sharing sleeping-quarters with Miles Carew, who admittedly had been around in the background at intervals all her life, but whom she'd known only very slightly up until last night. Now, after only a little more than twenty-four hours, she was beginning to feel she knew Miles better than anyone else in the world.

Which was what danger and crisis did for one, she decided as she settled down in the bed in his dressing-room. This was probably what people experienced in wartime, why relationships were stripped down to the essentials so quickly. Whether she liked Miles Carew or not, one thing was certain. She had no qualms about her personal safety as long as he was near. And she did like him. Not in the same way as Harry, or Mark, either. Now that the awe Miles had once inspired was gone, her feelings for him were nothing remotely like her affection for his younger brothers.

She listened, but heard nothing until a soft tap on the door heralded Miles's presence.

'Elinor?' he whispered.

'I'm asleep,' she whispered back, chuckling.

'Good,' he said severely. 'Stay that way until morning, please.'

'Yes, sir.'

He laughed. 'Goodnight.'

Elinor woke with a start, thinking it must be daylight, then realised the security lights outside were shining through her curtains. She jumped out of bed and ran to the door, colliding with Miles, who was coming the other way.

'No panic,' he said quickly, and pulled her across the room to the window, where the curtains were drawn back. 'There's the culprit.'

Elinor caught her breath as she saw a chunky dark shape moving slowly across the snow-covered terrace. 'A badger! I've never actually seen one before.'

'There's a set down over the cliff; he must be going home.'

She let out a long, shaky breath. 'Lovely as our friend Brock is, I wish he'd stay there under the circumstances. I thought it was our friend on the move.'

'If it had been we wouldn't have seen him,' Miles informed her.

Elinor turned round, startled, pushing her untidy hair back from her face. 'Why not?'

'Because, as I said before, something tells me he's someone trained in the same line of business as me—an old hand at covering his tracks.' He took her by the arm. 'Come on, back to bed. You're frozen.'

Despite her warm pyjamas Elinor was shivering from head to foot by the time he insisted on tucking her into bed, though whether it was from mere cold or at the thought of a highly trained member of the Special Services out to harass them was hard to tell.

Miles, looming tall in a long dark wool dressing-gown, stood looking down at her by the light of the small lamp he'd switched on. 'Would you like a hot drink?'

She shook her head, violently against the idea of Miles leaving her vicinity, even to go downstairs. 'No, thanks, I'll soon be warm. Thanks for showing me the badger.'

'Better than letting you imagine all kinds of faceless horrors.'

'Very true,' she admitted, and smiled up at him. 'Goodnight—not that there's that much left of it by this time.'

'No. So make the most of it. Shall I close the door?'

She shook her head. 'No—please.'

'What if I snore?'

'You haven't so far.'

'So you didn't get to sleep very quickly after all!' He switched off the light. 'Try to get some rest, Elinor. Then tomorrow I drive you back, and no argument.'

'Goodnight again,' she said, avoiding a direct answer, and lay very still, reassured by the minimal sounds she heard as he got into bed in the other room. He did everything very quietly, as she would have expected from someone versed in his particular form of warfare. She shivered as she faced the fact that their faceless enemy was similarly skilful if Miles's suspicions were correct.

To her amazement she woke next morning to find that she'd slept soundly after all. She sat up in bed and peered through the curtains, her eyes widening as she looked out on a whirling white wilderness. In the night the snow had returned with a vengeance.

She leapt out of bed and pulled on several layers of clothes, shivering despite the warmth from the radiator beside the bed. Taking a peep into the main bedroom, to find it empty and clinically tidy, she hurried to the bathroom with her wash-bag, then ran downstairs to the kitchen a few minutes later to find Miles at the kitchen table, the same scents of coffee and toast in the air as the day before.

'Good morning.' He jumped up to pull out a chair for her. 'Did you sleep well?'

'Surprisingly, yes—and a lot longer than intended,' she said apologetically, and smiled diffidently, struck anew by the strangeness of the situation. 'Sorry I'm late.'

'Why?' He passed the toast-rack to her. 'No rush this morning. No chance of driving back to Cheltenham today, Elinor. I'll need a mammoth session of shovelling to clear the garage doors, and even if I get the Range Rover out it won't be much use. According to travel bulletins on the radio the main road's blocked in several places. Until this lot lets up apparently there's not much hope of getting through.'

Elinor poured herself a cup of coffee, not in the least dismayed by this piece of news. 'So you're stuck with me for the time being.' She smiled at him over the steaming cup. 'Bad luck, Miles. At least I can help you shovel.'

Miles, looking tough and efficient in khakis with a heavy tabbed sweater, eyed her up and down with a faint grin. '*Can* you shovel?'

'Can I?' she said with derision. 'I've lived here all my life, remember. It doesn't snow very often in these parts, but when it does it makes a thorough job of it. I remember the burst pipes at Cliff Cottage a few years ago. Mother had to get new carpet fitted everywhere upstairs.'

'So your father told me.' Miles stared through the window bleakly. 'In any case there's not much point in trying to clear any snow while it's still coming down like this.'

'And I don't imagine your friend will try anything in this weather either,' said Elinor cheerfully, then sobered at the look on Miles's face. 'You don't agree,' she added, crestfallen.

'No point in deluding you, Elinor. If he's what I think he is snow won't worry him in the slightest. It might even be a help.'

She blew out her cheeks. 'So there's nothing we can do?'

He shook his head. 'No more than we're doing already. I've made the house as secure as possible, we're in contact with the outside world, Sophie's safe and you, at least, are now where I can keep an eye on you.'

Elinor considered this, then nodded briskly. 'Right. Shall I make another pot of coffee?'

He smiled a little. 'Of course. Do whatever you want, as long as you don't go out of doors.'

'In this weather?' she said, grinning back, and went over to fill the kettle.

By the time they'd eaten bacon and eggs for lunch the snow had stopped. Miles listened to the latest radio weather forecast then got up quickly.

'Time I got busy with a shovel!'

'Give me five minutes to clear away and I'll be with you,' said Elinor promptly.

'I'd rather you didn't.' He eyed her, frowning, as he pulled on a waterproof wind-cheater. 'I'd feel happier if you stayed in the house.'

'And I'll feel happier if I come with you,' she retorted, determination in every line of her as she stacked plates in the dishwasher. Please, Miles. If I help I'll feel I'm earning my keep. Besides, I need occupation.'

'All right,' he agreed reluctantly. 'There's an old parka of Harry's on the hook. Your boots will have to do.'

'They certainly won't spoil—they're ancient!'

'Nevertheless, they're likely to be ruined,' Miles warned.

'I'll change them the moment we come in,' she promised, and drew on the woollen gloves he'd dried for her. 'Right. Lead on Major. Private Gibson reporting for duty.'

'No army private ever looked like you,' he assured her, grinning at the picture she made in Harry's jacket, which reached almost to her knees.

Elinor rolled up the sleeves a little, undeterred. 'I'll be a big help nevertheless.'

Armed with shovels, they slithered over deep snow on the way down to the garage. It had been a coach-house in days gone by and stood in a horseshoe of trees ringed by a laurel hedge. Normally it was sheltered from the prevailing westerlies which blew up the River Wye, but the snow had been driven in overnight on a north-easterly and great drifts blocked the double wooden garage doors to shoulder height.

The pair set to with a will, but in spite of Miles's strength and fitness and Elinor's enthusiasm it soon became obvious that the task was beyond a mere shovel, no matter who handled it.

'No use,' he panted after a while. 'This is a job for machinery. I'll ring the farm and ask one of the Morgan boys to come up and dig us out.'

By the time they'd made their way back up the steep rise to the big yard behind the house, Elinor was thankful to yield her shovel to Miles as he unlocked the door. She stamped snow off her boots before going in, then stripped off the parka with relief, amazed at the heat it had kept in during her shovelling.

Miles kicked off his boots, then went into the kitchen to fetch her shoes.

'Thank you,' she said, still breathing hard. 'I wouldn't have believed I could get so hot out in that—a pity it was all for nothing.'

'You did amazingly well,' he assured her, 'but no one could shift that lot without help. I'll ring the farm.' He picked up the phone, listened, and frowned. 'Probably something wrong with this thing—I'll use the one in the study.' When he came back to the kitchen his face was grim. 'The line's dead.'

'And the electricity's off,' said Elinor, biting her lip. 'I just tried to switch on the kettle.'

Their eyes met for an instant then Miles made a dash for the study again. From the front windows there was a view of the farm far below, and the houses dotted along the winding length of Springfield Lane. The sullen sky was already growing dark. Dark enough to show lights gleaming in most of the houses.

Miles stared down at them, face set, and a cold shiver dispatched Elinor's glow as she reached him. 'We're on the same circuit as those houses down there,' he said grimly. 'I think we've just embarked on phase two of our friend's war of nerves.'

'So what now?' she asked, trying hard to sound cheerful.

'I get myself down the lane to the farm at top speed, so I can report the faults—not that any maintenance men will get through in this weather,' he added, frowning. 'But at least I can get my name on the list, and ask one of the Morgan boys for a hand to clear the snow.'

'Right. I'll come with you.'

'Normally I wouldn't hear of it, but under the circumstances I'd rather have you under my eye, as close to me as possible,' he said as they dressed for the weather again.

'My sentiments exactly,' she agreed with fervour.

Miles frowned. 'Of course, I could ask Mrs Morgan at the farm to put you up, or take you on down to your Mrs Crouch.'

'No fear!' said Elinor incensed. 'Unless,' she added, lifting her chin, 'you'd rather have me off your hands, of course.'

'That's not the point,' he said brusquely. 'Frankly, I'd insist if it weren't for the risk involved.'

She frowned. 'Risk?'

'If you're here with me I can protect you. If you transfer somewhere else it's just possible that our man may turn his attentions to the new location.'

'You mean put Mrs C in danger if she takes me in?'

'Exactly.'

'No way—I'll stay here,' said Elinor forcibly, then eyed him, frowning. 'If that's all right with you?'

He gave her a wry grin. 'I don't seem to have much choice. Come on, let's get down to the farm and back at the double. I want you safe and sound in here again before dark.'

By the time they'd battled through the thick snow leading to the farm half a mile down Springfield Lane, asked the eldest Morgan son to report the fault to the electricity board, requested help with the tractor next day, then battled up the steep road to Cliff House, Elinor was more tired than she'd have believed possible.

'I go to aerobics classes twice a week,' she gasped as they reached the back door. 'I fondly imagined I was fit!'

Miles, apparently unaffected by the gruelling pace he'd set for the expedition, hurried her into the dark house and locked the door behind them. 'Sorry I pushed you so hard. I want the camping-stove set up and candles everywhere before it gets too dark to see.' He went into the big, old-fashioned larder, and made a couple of journeys into the kitchen with a two-burner gas stove, several boxes of candles and two large rubber torches. 'The gas cylinder is up in the tool-shed,' he said as Elinor lit candles and stuck them on saucers. 'I won't be a minute.'

She bit back a plea to go with him. 'Right,' she said brightly. 'I could murder a cup of tea.'

He went outside, locking the outer door behind him, and Elinor, torch in hand, found a saucepan and filled it with water, ready to heat when he got back with the gas. It seemed a long, long time before he did. Her nerves were jangling long before he reappeared with the cylinder.

'Sorry I took so long,' he said, connecting it to the lead from the stove. 'Our visitor's been in the tool-shed.'

Elinor stared at him in dismay, heart thumping. 'How do you know?'

'Various things were fractionally out of place.' He put a match to one of the burners and took the pan of water she handed him. 'Which means he left them like that deliberately to show me he's been there. And since I took the shovels out earlier on, at that,' he added.

'You mean he'd have covered his tracks otherwise?'

'Right. Now the telephone's out of commission he can't keep up the phone calls, so this is his way of reminding me he's in charge.' He slammed a lid on the pan angrily.

'Forgive me for saying so,' said Elinor, 'but you don't suppose he's been in here too, as well as the tool-shed?'

Miles shook his head. 'I doubt it. So far he's done nothing that anyone can prove. But if I catch him breaking and entering it's a police matter. And whoever this maniac is he doesn't want that. He just wants to scare the living daylights out of me—and you too now you've joined the cast.'

'Would you think me a terrible coward if I asked you to look through the house just the same?' Elinor asked apologetically.

Miles gave her a searching look, shook his head and turned off the gas. 'No, Nell, of course I wouldn't. Come on, then; grab a torch and let's go hunting.'

Grateful for his forbearance, she stuck to him like glue as they searched the ground-floor rooms, then went upstairs to check every bedroom and bathroom, every cupboard, nook and cranny which might possibly house an intruder. At the head of the stairs, just when Elinor was reassured that no one could possibly be hidden anywhere, Miles reached inside an

airing cupboard for a hooked pole, opened the hatch
to the attic space and brought down a folding ladder.

'Might as well go the whole hog,' he said, 'but this
time stay where you are, Elinor.' He shone the torch
on her face and she nodded obediently, her heart in
her throat as Miles climbed the ladder and disappeared into the dark shadows of the roof space. She
heard him moving about, opening boxes and moving
things around, before he finally came back into view
and swung himself down.

'All clear.' He returned the ladder and hatch to their
original places, but took the pole with him as they
went downstairs. 'No point in making things easier
for him if he does take to breaking and entering.'

'You talk as if you know him,' commented Elinor,
feeling a lot better as they reached the candlelit
kitchen, which seemed like a familiar haven after the
shadowy spaces in the rest of the house.

'I'm positive I do—or did, at some time.' He relit
the gas burner and turned towards her. 'The man
doing this obviously has some kind of personal grudge
against me, so I must know him.'

'So what do we do now?' she asked as she made
tea by candlelight.

'Until the weather lets up, not a lot,' he said
brusquely. 'For myself I don't give a damn, but...'

'But with me on your hands it makes life difficult
for you,' she said, resigned. 'Sorry to mess things up.'

Miles's saturnine face softened slightly as they sat
down at the kitchen table. 'You haven't, Nell—just
complicated things slightly. I warn you it's going to
get cold here extremely quickly without any heating
on. Luckily the fires are made up everywhere. I'll light
the one in the study in a minute and raid the other

fireplaces for logs. There's a full log basket in the dining-room, too. Tom left that ready before he went.'

'And I can cook something on that stove of yours,' she said philosophically, determined to make the best of things.

'Good girl.' He drained his cup and got up. 'I'll light that fire, and if you take a look in one of the drawers over there you should find some batteries for the radio. I'd like to stay in touch with the outside world.'

Elinor was in complete agreement. She wouldn't have admitted it to Miles, but she felt horribly defenceless alone in the large kitchen. There were curtains on the windows on one side of the room, but none over the sink. She felt like a goldfish in a bowl, convinced she was being watched as she searched for batteries. But once she had the transistor working she felt better. The mere sound of music and voices introduced a feeling of normality, giving her courage as she searched cupboards for possible ideas for dinner. With only two gas burners at her command it soon became obvious that their meal would be basic in the extreme.

'How do you fancy sausages, mashed potatoes and canned baked beans?' she asked Miles, when he came to tell her that the study fire was doing nicely.

'Sounds good to me.' His teeth gleamed white in his dark face as he went to the sink to wash his hands. 'I've eaten a lot worse, in a lot dodgier circumstances, too.'

'I can imagine.'

'I doubt if you can!'

Elinor studied his slim, erect back thoughtfully. 'Were you sorry to leave the army, Miles?'

'In most ways, yes. It was like being part of a large family. I tend to feel a bit out in the cold sometimes, now I've resigned. But in future there's Sophie to think of, and a project I'm putting into operation. Until our man began putting in his nasty little oar I was pretty pleased with life. I should have remembered Murphy's law,' he finished savagely, turning round. 'Everything that can go wrong *will* go wrong.'

He let out an exasperated sigh. 'The trouble with this joker is that he knows he's got me over a barrel. Normally I'd go outside, check what's happened to the electricity supply and the telephone wires—but he knows damn well I'm vulnerable. If I'm outside with a torch I'm a target. And if anything happens to me— even just a knock on the head—you're in here alone, even more vulnerable.'

'A responsibility you could do without,' agreed Elinor sounding depressed.

He smiled suddenly. 'Unexpected, but the pleasure of your company far outweighs any disadvantage.'

'Now you're being polite!'

'What does it take to convince you?' He put an arm round her shoulders. 'It's a pleasure to renew our acquaintance, Miss Gibson. I would have preferred more favourable circumstances, but otherwise I've no complaint.'

She stood very still for a moment under the light, impersonal touch, then made for the camping-stove. 'If you want to dine reasonably early, Major Carew, I'd better make a start right now. I'm not used to cooking with gas, bottled or otherwise.'

However, the meal was ready sooner than Elinor expected, owing to Miles's efficient help. While she peeled potatoes he found a pan for the sausages and opened tins, both of them listening for updates on the weather, which was snarling up traffic nationwide with the heaviest snowfall of the winter.

'Where do you suppose your friend's hiding out?' said Elinor, once they were eating their meal.

'Could be anywhere. I don't envy him being out on a night like this, but if my guess is right he'll be used to it. I've survived far worse conditions on the Brecon Beacons, during training.'

'You don't think he'll have given up and taken himself off to a hotel for the night, then?'

'No, I don't.' Miles looked up from his plate to meet her eyes squarely. 'He's cut off our electricity and our means of communication, remember. He hasn't gone to that trouble for nothing.'

'So what do you think's next on the programme?'

'I wish I knew. But as I don't I vote we spend the rest of the evening as pleasantly as possible in the study where it's warm—and pray hard for a thaw.'

All in favour of this programme, Elinor decided it was time to behave like a guest and asked for news of Mark and Harry, then went on to draw Miles out on the subject of Sophie. He was only too happy to oblige, and by tacit consent they avoided further discussion of their faceless enemy as they finished their makeshift dinner. Once the meal was cleared away, Miles joined Elinor in the candlelit study, piled more logs on the fire and sat back in the worn leather chair completely at ease, as though this were something they did every night of their lives.

Elinor smiled at her thoughts and Miles offered her a penny for them.

'I was just thinking how comfortable we must look to the casual observer, not a bit like virtual prisoners.'

'Not for long. Tomorrow, once it's daylight,' said Miles, holding out his cup for more coffee, 'I intend to search every inch of the garden.'

'I still think you should inform the police,' she said flatly.

'Not yet, Elinor. I want to catch this man myself, find out who the devil he is and why he's making me a target.' His face hardened to a cold, hostile mask. 'No one threatens my family—or my friends—and gets away with it.'

Elinor felt chilled by the sudden glimpse behind his urbane façade. 'Won't it be awkward if you find you *do* know him, whoever he is?'

'Only for him,' he said grimly.

There was silence between them against the background of a Chopin prelude on Classic FM on the radio. A log split in two suddenly, startling Elinor, and Miles got up to kick the fire together and add more logs. He turned to her with a wry smile.

'Don't worry. I'll keep you safe.'

'I'm not in the least worried on that score,' she said with complete truth. 'I suppose I just can't believe it's happening—not to me, anyway. My life's normally a tad uneventful.'

He sat down again, eyeing her with interest. 'I've been so wrapped up in my own affairs I haven't even asked what you do for a living, Elinor.'

She gave a depressed sigh. 'I'm a legal secretary in a firm in Cheltenham.'

'Why the sigh? Don't you enjoy your work?'

'Actually I do, very much. Mother and Dad always wanted me to go in for medicine—naturally enough— but I was never that way inclined. I did a business studies course instead.'

'So what's the problem?'

She twisted a bright lock of hair round her finger, pulling a face as she gazed into the fire. 'Oliver's the solicitor I work for.'

Miles whistled. 'So you were going to marry your boss.'

She nodded morosely. 'And now I'm not, so goodbye job.'

'Why? Surely he won't sack you?'

'He won't have to. The moment I get back I'll resign.'

'So you've burned your boats, Elinor Gibson.'

'Afraid so.' She turned her eyes on him. 'But I wasn't acting on impulse in this instance. It's been coming ever since Christmas. The other night it finally came to a head. A friend of mine invited us to a party, but at the last minute Oliver told me he'd been asked to dine with an influential contact and wanted me to go too. I blew my top, asked why we never spent time with people just because we liked them. Every time something was arranged with any of my friends Oliver always had some excuse. Suddenly it became clear that life with him held out little promise of fun. I admit he's quite a bit older than me,' she added, 'but——'

'How much older?' Miles interrupted, looking curious.

'He's forty-one.' Elinor's eyes danced. 'Four years older than you, Miles.'

'A veritable greybeard!'

Elinor ran an impersonal eye over her companion's spare frame. Even in repose it was obvious that Miles Carew was supremely fit, without a superfluous ounce of flesh on his slim, athletic body. Not one grey hair frosted the gleaming dark hair, and the fine lines at the corners of his eyes somehow suggested habitual scanning of far horizons rather than advance warnings of age. Oliver Maynard was equally tall, but his greying auburn hair was beginning to recede and, Elinor acknowledged with sudden insight, he had the sleek look of a man fond of good food and vintage wines.

'Not so,' she disagreed, lips twitching. 'But now you come to mention it he does look rather more than four years older than you, Major.'

'I wonder if I should take that as a compliment?' said Miles, eyes narrowed.

She laughed. 'Oh, definitely. Oliver looks exactly what he is—a man in his early forties—whereas in most ways you seem a lot less than twelve years older than me!'

'Definitely a compliment. Thank you, Miss Gibson.' He looked at her curiously. 'You said "most ways". What's the exception?'

'When you think about getting your hands on our intruder you look like a cold, grim stranger.'

'You have problems with that?'

'Not exactly. I just hope I never see that look turned on me!'

He gave her his sudden, transforming smile. 'I doubt I could ever feel cold and grim where you're concerned, Elinor.'

A little put out to find that her pulse was racing, she returned the smile rather coolly. 'I'm relieved. Though once this—this business is over I won't be coming this way again once my parents move to Monmouth.'

'Not even if invited? I'd take it as a favour if you came to see Sophie occasionally. It's bound to feel a little strange to her at first, until she integrates with the children at school.'

Elinor smiled, surprised. 'Then of course I'll come.'

'Good.' Miles gave her an odd, wry look. 'After all, you'll feel very much at home.'

'After surviving the siege here with you?'

'I meant at Cliff Cottage. I asked your father to keep it under his hat until the contracts were signed, but you may as well know he's sold the house to me.'

Elinor stared at him in blank astonishment. '*Really*? But why on earth do you want the cottage, Miles, when you've got this place?'

'For Sophie and me to live in. I hope to turn Cliff House into a paying proposition.'

'A hotel?'

'Not quite. It's in a unique position on top of the cliff with the river below, which makes it the ideal place for those leadership courses multinationals subject their executives to these days. I know all about physical endurance courses. I also know a few ex-army chaps I'd like to put in employment.' Miles looked suddenly poker-faced. 'And in school holidays I'd like to get inner-city kids here, give them the benefit of good Wye Valley air.'

'Subsidised by the fees from the leadership courses?'

'More or less. Soon work's going to start on restoration of the old tennis courts, and I'm building a combined gym and swimming-pool in what used to be the walled garden. Planning permission's just come through,' he added with satisfaction.

Elinor gazed at him, deeply impressed. 'But won't that take an awful lot of money?'

Miles smiled crookedly. 'After the divorce, when Selina had legally given Sophie into my care, my godfather died. He was a bit of an entrepreneur, old Godfrey, had his fingers in all sorts of pies; he was a real charmer too. I was very fond of him—used to dine with him at his club when I was on leave. He and Selina never got on, so I gave up trying to take her along years ago, but he adored Sophie—took her to tea at the Ritz not long before he died.

'My father always said Godfrey Pargeter was comfortably off, but I honestly never knew the old boy was so loaded. To me he was just someone I was very fond of, and not just because he sent me expensive presents on my birthday and stood me to slap-up meals. He took his duties as godfather very seriously; he used to come down to Winchester and watch when I played cricket, came to my passing-out parade at Sandhurst and so on. He was like a father in that respect after my own father died. I thought the world of him.'

'It was obviously mutual. He left you some money, I take it.'

'He left me a lot of money, Elinor. Some of it's in trust for Sophie until she comes of age, and there were several bequests to charities, but I got the lion's share, with an odd sort of proviso. Godfrey made a request in his will that I should put the money to good use, in whatever way I saw fit.'

'He obviously knew you well, because it sounds as though you're doing exactly that,' commented Elinor in approval. 'It's a brilliant idea, Miles. Will you be involved in running the place?'

'With the help of an accountant I'll do the admin work. Otherwise I'm bringing in some men recently retired from the regiment to supervise the activity side of things, and I've lined up a couple of teachers for the summer school.'

'It all sounds wonderful—I don't suppose you've got a job for me?' she said, meaning it as a joke.

'If you mean that I'm in crying need of a secretary already, before I've even started, yes!' He waved a hand at the litter of paperwork covering the table. 'You'd be doing me an enormous favour if you helped me out with that, if only for a while.'

Elinor flushed. 'I really meant it as a joke, but if you're serious I might take it on at that,' she said, warming to the idea. 'Until you move into Cliff Cottage, of course. After that I'll have nowhere to live in Stavely.'

'We'll meet that obstacle when we come to it,' he said swiftly, and jumped to his feet, holding out his hand. 'Well? Shall we shake on it, Elinor? I warn you it's likely to be chaos here for the next few months, but if you're willing to tackle it with me I'll be deeply in your debt. To prove it I'll pay ten per cent more than whatever you get now as salary.'

'Very generous.' Elinor got up and put her hand in his. 'But let's have a trial period to start with—see how we get on.'

Miles smiled at her. 'Good idea. You might find me impossible to work with.'

'And vice versa,' she pointed out.

Miles tightened his grip, the smile missing as his eyes held hers. 'That I find hard to visualise, Elinor.'

CHAPTER FOUR

THIS time as they went upstairs together Elinor felt less at ease, and knew intuitively that Miles felt the same. She hurried through her preparations for the night in the picturesque bathroom, then wished him a rather subdued goodnight as she shut herself into his dressing-room.

Last night, she realised as she dived into bed, Miles had still seemed very much the younger Carews' elder brother, someone she held in slight awe. Tonight things were different. This crisis-type atmosphere was acting like a hothouse on their relationship, she thought, frowning. If they were really going to work together in the future—and she liked the idea enormously—things had to be kept on the old footing, where she was Harry's and Mark's playmate from the cottage and he was Major Carew from Cliff House.

As she tried to relax enough to fall asleep, it occurred to her that tonight, at least, there would be no security lights to wake her when Brock the badger set off on his nightly outing.

She woke instead to an unearthly scream somewhere outside in the night, and shot up in bed, heart pounding. Before she could think better of it instinct sent her racing for the door in the pitch-darkness to get to Miles, who, to her astonishment, appeared to be sleeping. She tiptoed across the room to wake him, then screamed her head off as a tall figure materialised in the doorway to the bathroom.

'Elinor!' yelled Miles, shaking her. 'It's me.' He held her tightly as she collapsed against his chest in shock, shaking from head to foot with fear and cold.

'I heard a scream,' she said hoarsely, clutching at him.

He shook her slightly, his voice indulgent. 'Surely a country-bred wench like you recognised a screech-owl?'

'No, I didn't; I thought—I don't know what I thought!' Elinor pulled away in embarrassment. 'Damn! I'm sorry, Miles; I'm not usually such a moron.'

'You're on edge, Nell—and no wonder. And it's an unearthly sound,' he added. 'Enough to frighten anyone.'

She sniffed, unappeased. 'I ought to have recognised an owl, just the same. But I really thought you were there in the bed.'

'I left the covers in a mound when I got up.'

'Why did you?' she demanded in sudden suspicion. 'Did you hear anything?'

He coughed. 'I'm afraid I'm subject to the calls of nature just like any other man, Elinor.'

'Oh! Oh, *sorry*,' she muttered, and scuttled into the dressing-room with a muffled goodnight, well aware that Miles was trying hard not to laugh.

This time she found it impossible to get to sleep. She tossed and turned in the narrow bed, every creak and groan of the old house magnified by her imagination into sounds of an intruder forcing entry to murder them both in their beds. After an hour or so of this she even began to hope it would thaw sufficiently to let her go back to her flat next day, even if it meant evicting Linda's boyfriend.

But that would mean leaving Miles alone. And that she couldn't do. The fact that he was a battle-hardened soldier, and ex-Special Forces at that, was entirely irrelevant. At this particular moment in time he needed support of some kind. Whoever this lunatic was she wouldn't be able to live with herself if she left Miles to face him alone.

Squinting at the luminous dial of her watch, she found it was still only three in the morning and a long time to go before the winter dawn. And, to add to her joys, a trip to the bathroom was becoming urgent. Heaving a sigh, she got to her feet, pulled on a sweater over her pyjamas and tiptoed to the door.

'Elinor?' said Miles instantly as she opened it. 'Something the matter?'

'I need to go to the bathroom,' she muttered.

'Use the torch beside my bed,' he ordered.

She collected it on her way past, went into the bathroom and closed the door behind her. When she got back Miles was on his feet, staring out of the window.

'Can you see anything?' she said nervously.

'No. Just snow and more snow. I wish this bloody thaw would hurry up.'

'Chris Morgan should be able to get the tractor up here tomorrow.' She shivered, and Miles turned swiftly.

'You're freezing!' he accused, and wrapped his arms round her, holding her in a light, impersonal embrace. As if she were his maiden aunt, she thought in sudden, rash resentment, and wriggled closer. The arms round her tightened instinctively, holding her so close that she felt sure he must be deafened by the sudden pounding of her heart.

For a long, throbbing moment they stood like statues, then he suddenly bent his head to kiss her. Their lips met, parted, then met again with sudden, mutual heat, the shock of it filling Elinor with a sensation which mounted rapidly to a hot, pulsing pleasure she'd never felt before. Blood raced through her veins in response to the deeply gratifying vibration in Miles's hard, warm body as he kissed her fiercely, his invading tongue inflammatory as he prolonged the embrace until she was a throbbing mass of quivering nerve-ends clamouring for something more.

Then his arms dropped suddenly and she felt cold and bereft as he stepped back, breathing hard.

'I shouldn't have done that,' he said hoarsely. 'I never imagined—oh, hell! Look, don't worry. You needn't be frightened, Elinor.'

'I'm not. Not in the least,' she assured him breathlessly.

He let out a harsh, ragged breath. 'Then you should be—and you know damn well why, too. Go to bed, Elinor. Now.'

After a night spent battling with embarrassment and several other warring emotions, Elinor finally fell into a doze shortly before first light and woke an hour later feeling like death warmed up. She swung her feet to the floor, eyeing the closed door morosely. The nocturnal episode with Miles was still so vivid in her mind that the last thing she fancied was coming face to face with him in the icy cold light of day. She dressed hurriedly, all fingers and thumbs, and drew back the curtains to look out at a relentlessly white world, then marched to the door, tapped on it and peered round it warily.

The bedroom was untenanted, the bed neatly made, the bathroom beyond empty. She heaved a sigh of relief and went through her morning routine on autopilot while she figured out how to deal with the situation so that Miles would realise she wasn't attaching any importance to it.

The worrying part was how he'd taken her no-holds-barred response. There had been a lot of kisses in her life. But none of them, not even Oliver's, had ever set her alight like those exchanged with Miles last night. His kisses had been different. Vastly different. He had lit fires deep inside her, fires it had taken hours to put out afterwards. Oliver was a practised, considerate lover, but the most she'd experienced in his arms was a temperate sort of pleasure, the very lukewarm aspect of it a hidden disappointment. That part of their relationship, short-lived though it had been, was something she wouldn't miss in the slightest.

But in Miles's arms the pleasure she'd felt was totally intemperate, an uninhibited response from every hormone in her body. Last night she'd discovered, at last, exactly what the man-woman fuss was all about.

Elinor, she told herself cynically, it was just a few kisses, the not unnatural result of danger and propinquity. Not the sweet mystery of life at all. No big deal. At least, it certainly won't have been to Miles. All you have to do is behave normally.

And on this sensible note Elinor went down to the kitchen prepared to greet Miles as though nothing had happened.

It was something of a let-down to find the kitchen cold and empty, with the table laid for one, and a note on her plate.

I've gone on a recce outside. Don't worry if I'm a while; there's a fair area to search. I've laid the fire in the study. Put a match to it. I've locked the door behind me. Don't open it to anyone until I get back.

The note was signed with a capital M, the handwriting decisive and unembellished. Like Miles, thought Elinor, thoroughly deflated, and switched on the radio, then put a match to one of the gas burners to boil water for tea.

She had finished the contents of the teapot, eaten a piece of bread and butter and read a three-day-old newspaper from cover to cover before she saw Miles striding along the cliff path towards the backyard. He peered in through the kitchen windows as he passed, then gave his usual tattoo on the outer door before unlocking it, stamping the snow from his boots then coming in to take off his parka.

'Good morning,' he said cheerfully, smiling at her as she hovered in the kitchen doorway. 'Did you light the fire?'

'Hi,' said Elinor brightly. 'I didn't, actually. Not much point until later—I thought we'd save on logs. I've put on an extra sweater and my boots instead. I've got some water boiling, though. Want some coffee?'

'Please.' He pulled on his desert boots and came into the kitchen. 'I went over every inch of the place, but no sign of our friend. Which doesn't surprise me.'

'Why?' said Elinor, pouring boiling water into two large mugs.

'I doubt he'd hole up on the property itself.' Miles shrugged. 'He might even be putting up somewhere at night, just as you said.'

'Any sign of a thaw?' asked Elinor as they sat down with their coffee.

'The forecast promises a rise in temperature later today,' he said, cradling his hands round his mug. 'Which means we may get some electricity by tonight—even the phone back on. I saw Denzil Morgan just now, passing by on his tractor; he said he'll be up mid-morning with Chris to dig us out. Apparently the trains are still on stop locally, and people are advised to keep off the roads unless absolutely necessary. The electricity board might make it, but I'm afraid you're stuck here for another day at least, Elinor.'

She took her courage in both hands and looked him in the eye. 'Is that a problem for you, Miles? After last night, I mean?'

He smiled in unexpected approval. 'Straight from the shoulder, Elinor. Good. And since you've brought the subject up I'd be lying if I denied that things took rather an unexpected turn in the night. But you have my word——'

'Word of an officer and a gentleman?'

He laughed. 'An outdated phrase, maybe, but as good as any. What I'm trying to say, as politely as possible, is that I've never been ruled by my basic instincts, Elinor, so don't worry, I shan't take advantage of the situation—or of you.'

She stared at him in surprise. 'It never occurred to me that you would. I just thought you'd be embarrassed, and want to get rid of me as quickly as possible.'

'You couldn't be more wrong. So neither of us need worry. Not on that subject, anyway.' He sobered. 'My main concern lies with our friend, and what's next on his agenda.'

'Perhaps he's given up.'

'I'd like to think so, but I doubt it.' He eyed the snow-covered landscape outside, frowning. 'Incidentally, I went down and looked round Cliff Cottage while I was out, and all seems well. I didn't go inside, obviously—perhaps we could do that later. But there's no sign of forced entry, apart from neatly cut electricity cables and a severed telephone line. He did the same up here. Everything was so damned accessible for him—the devil didn't even need a ladder. A pair of insulated cutters—or maybe just heavily insulated gloves—and bull's-eye! He's cut us off from the world.'

He looked up as loud knocking sounded on the outer door, and shot a reassuring glance at Elinor as she tensed visibly. 'It's all right, Nell—the Morgans to the rescue.'

Feeling rather silly, Elinor decided that she would stay in the house and prepare lunch while Miles went off to help with the snow-clearing.

'Are you sure you'll be all right?' he said, frowning as he got into his parka. 'I don't like leaving you alone.'

She smiled. 'You don't need me and my trusty shovel today, so I might as well concoct some soup or something and make myself useful up here instead of watching you toil. It's mid-morning, broad daylight and I'll lock myself in. I'll be fine.'

Obviously reluctant, Miles finally went off, armed with a spade, and Elinor locked the door after him; then, just to reassure herself, she went on a quick tour of the house. Though what, she thought wryly, she would do if she came face to face with an intruder wasn't clear.

Nevertheless she felt happier once she'd checked, and back in the kitchen, with the radio for company, she chopped leeks, celery, carrots and potatoes, and put them with the ham bone to simmer. Then, to her delight, a lightning search through Mrs Hedley's freezer not only produced lamb chops, but some neatly labelled packets of frozen herbs, which meant mint sauce with their dinner later and parsley dumplings with the lunchtime soup.

Elinor smiled to herself as she sat down with a cup of coffee. A few days ago she wouldn't have believed her eyes if they'd seen into the future and showed her at Cliff House, cooking lunch for the man who'd been the object of her youthful hero-worship. Life was full of little surprises. Big ones too, she thought, haunted by last night's kisses.

A little later, after she'd tidied the study, she was looking for a book to read when she heard a knock on the back door, and went to answer it.

'Who is it?' she called.

'Miss Gibson? It's the electricity board, madam,' said a cheery voice. 'Mr Carew said you'd let me in to check the junction boxes in the downstairs hallway.'

Elinor unlocked the door, eyed the friendly man in a donkey jacket, glanced at the identification he showed her, then motioned him inside.

'Through here,' she said, leading the way from the kitchen to the hall. 'Does this mean we'll have power soon?'

'Not exactly.'

Before Elinor could turn in enquiry her hands were seized and pulled behind her back, the mouth she opened to scream gagged by a hard, merciless hand.

'Co-operate and you won't get hurt,' said the man in her ear. 'No point in screaming. The dashing major's down by the garage, directing operations as usual.'

Elinor, petrified with fear, stayed still in the cruel grasp, her arms wrenched back in an iron-hard grip. The hand left her mouth to knot itself tightly in her hair, straining her head back.

'Listen,' rasped the voice in her ear. 'You're coming with me, straight out of the front door and along the cliff.'

'He'll come after us,' gasped Elinor, trying to twist so that she could look her captor in the face.

'Keep still!' he snarled, then let out the soft chuckle she'd heard on the phone. 'Of course he'll come after us. That's the object of the exercise.'

'I'm cold. I need a coat——'

'No time for that. You'll survive—if you co-operate.' The hand released her hair, but only to secure her wrists while her assailant spun her round to face him, holding up a knife before her wide, horrified eyes. The man was nothing like the monster of her imagination, she saw, trembling. He was about the same build as Miles, with similar dark hair, but his prominent eyes were like blank blue pebbles. His lips curved in cold triumph as he waved the knife gently under her chin. 'Persuasion enough?'

Elinor nodded convulsively, shamed by her own fear.

'*Very* sensible.' The smile widened. 'What a perfect little decoy you make, my dear. The gallant major will come charging to the rescue—and then we'll see who's in command!'

Gripping her wrists together in one bruising hand, the man thrust her along the hall, reached round to unlock the front door, then propelled her outside, closing the door quietly behind him.

'Right,' he said. 'There's a path along the cliff here. Don't try any fancy stuff or you'll fall down a few hundred feet of limestone face to the Wye.'

Elinor felt a leap of exultation. The man might know Miles, but he didn't realise she'd had the run of the Cliff House acres as a child too. The cliffs might be limestone, but in places there were bushes and trees on sloping gradients before the sheer drop to the river.

He manhandled her along the narrow twisting path in the cold bright light of midday, through a glittering, disintegrating landscape as snow thawed and melted and lumps of it crashed from the trees that lined the edge. He pushed her along at a punishing pace and Elinor gasped painfully as the icy air knifed through her chest and her heart pounded from exertion and fear. Several times her feet slipped on the thawing surface in her crêpe-soled boots and the man cursed and hauled her upright as they reached the narrowest stretch of path, which led towards the gazebo built the previous century to give a view of the River Wye and its serpentine bends.

'Not so fast. I—I can't keep my balance,' she panted hoarsely. 'Please—I'm terrified of falling. I get vertigo.'

'Too bad,' he said, unmoved.

'I won't be much use as a decoy if I'm dead,' she pleaded, playing for time desperately. 'I can't bear the thought of falling down there.' She glanced down at the drop and shut her eyes tightly, shuddering, but the man tightened his bruising grip on her wrists as he started off again, dragging her with him.

Suddenly the man stumbled on an outcrop of rock masked by snow. Elinor, keyed up to take even a half-chance to escape, gave herself no time to think, tearing herself from his loosened grasp to go hurtling deliberately over the cliff. She rolled over and over, winded and gasping, then, with an involuntary scream, shot from sight down a drop which looked sheer from above but which catapulted her into the safe embrace of a sturdy clump of snow-masked bushes which broke her fall on one of the gradients, just as she'd calculated.

Shaking from head to foot with shock and fright, winded, her heart banging against her ribs, she lay as still as she could for a moment, praying her captor wouldn't come after her. Then she began to inch into the heart of the bushes and lay prone while her heart slowed a little and air heaved into her lungs.

Her mind worked furiously. If her calculations were right, a few more feet down to her right there was a cave—not much of a cave, more of an overhang of rock forming a crevice masked by bushes and small trees. She'd spent many a happy hour huddled in it with Harry and Mark in years gone by, acting out all kinds of melodramatic scenarios.

She listened, but there was no sound of someone coming to her rescue—or to recapture her. The man probably thought she was lying dead on the rocks below. Which rather fouled up the decoy idea. Though when Miles got back to the house and found her missing he'd come after her anyway. She clenched her teeth, hoping he was armed with the knife he'd used on her that first night—so short a time ago, she realised, feeling as though she'd lived a whole lifetime since running for cover to Cliff Cottage.

But who on earth was the mystery man! He was no lout. He spoke with the accent of an expensive education, like Miles. She breathed in deeply. Whoever he was she had no intention of letting him catch her again.

Cautiously she began to wriggle down the slope on her stomach, desperately frightened of falling now that the rush of adrenalin had receded. Reaction was setting in fast and she shivered as the snow soaked her, chilling her to the bone. She edged fearfully from one bush to another, stopping each time to listen, but there were no sounds of pursuit. She reached a pair of stunted trees, praying they were a landmark she was looking for, then, summoning every last scrap of courage she possessed, she slithered down over an outcrop of rock and lay still again.

After a minute or two she pushed through a clump of snow-covered bushes and almost cried with relief as she reached the tiny cave that Harry and Mark called the Hide. Wriggling in until the bushes concealed her from the world outside, she put her head down on her knees and locked her arms round them, every sobbing breath a pain in her chest as she fought to calm down.

Now that she was safe from him, if only for a while, she burned with shame, despite her shivering, mortified because her attacker had terrified her into obeying him so spinelessly. She hugged her arms across her chest, wondering what to do next. For a while she'd have to stay where she was, though if she didn't get out of here soon she was likely to suffer from hypothermia very quickly at this rate, thaw or no thaw. The cave was like a miniature deep-freeze, and very dirty. Her heavy white Aran sweater would never be the same again.

Suddenly Elinor tensed as sounds came from above on the cliff path. She could hear raised voices. One of them was Miles's voice, she realised, brightening, the cold rage in it easily discernible, even at this distance, in the clear, still air. He'd obviously come face to face with his tormentor at last.

She pressed her hands to her mouth, wishing desperately that she knew what was happening on the cliff path, then she heard a gun go off and smothered a shriek of horror. She got to her knees, trembling from head to foot as she heard someone descending the slopes from the cliff path at breakneck speed. The man had shot Miles, and now he was coming after her!

Elinor looked round wildly in the gloom, then found a rock and held it ready as someone dropped down the overhang of sheltering rock. Hands thrust aside the curtain of bushes and, on the point of letting fly with her missile, she saw the haggard, anguished face of Miles Carew. The rock dropped from her hand and she hurtled herself into his arms.

'God, how I prayed you'd be in here! Are you all right? Did the bastard harm you?' he demanded, panting as he crushed her to him, and she shook her head, burrowing her face into his shoulder.

'No, no! Is he dead?' she sobbed. 'Did you shoot him?'

Miles gave a bark of laughter. 'Hell, no, that was Denzil Morgan with his shotgun—fired it over our friend's head to bring an end to the proceedings.'

'Was the man afraid Denzil would really shoot him, then?'

'No. Denzil thought *I* was going to commit murder, and put a stop to it.'

'Where's the man now?'

'In the kitchen at the house, with a very excited Chris Morgan helping his father stand guard over him.'

Elinor let out a deep, shaky breath. 'What a stupid, stupid fool I was. I'm so *sorry*, Miles. He said he was from the electricity board, greeted me by name, even flashed one of those identification cards at me. He told me you'd said he was to come in to look at the junction boxes.'

'Captain Alexander Reid is—or was—an old friend of mine, or so I thought,' said Miles grimly.

'He's in the *army*?' said Elinor incredulously.

'Not any more. But explanations can wait. Time to get you back up the cliff and into some dry clothes. Your teeth are chattering like castanets. Do you think you can make it?'

'Of course I can,' she said scornfully, ready for anything now their phantom intruder was in custody. 'I've been up and down here hundreds of times.'

Miles nodded, his face grim. 'I pinned my hopes on that. Even so, when Reid said you'd fallen over the cliff I went berserk. Good job the Morgans were with me.'

'But you wouldn't have killed him really, Miles—would you?' she asked as he hoisted her up the overhang.

'No. Sandy Reid's not worth serving time for!' Miles swung himself up beside her then took her hand. 'I just wanted to *half* kill him, for taking off with you.'

CHAPTER FIVE

THE scene they walked in on in the kitchen at Cliff House was so like an old B-movie that at any other time Elinor would have laughed. Alexander Reid was sitting in a kitchen chair with his hands tied behind his back, one eye half closed and starting to discolour, blood seeping from a swollen split lip. Chris Morgan, who was six feet four and played lock forward for the local rugby team, hovered over him menacingly, obviously hoping the captive would offer some resistance. Chris's father, Denzil, built on the same lines as his son, leaned negligently at the kitchen counter, his shotgun broken over his arm, looking relaxed by contrast, yet something about him indicating very clearly that the outnumbered Mr Reid would be a fool to attempt anything rash.

And though her acquaintance with Alexander Reid was slight—if memorable—Elinor felt sure he was anything but a fool.

Miles gave her no time to further her acquaintance with the prisoner. She was allowed only a quick word of thanks to the Morgans before he hustled her out of the room and up the stairs, ordering her to get in a hot bath and find some dry clothes.

'What are you going to do to him?' she asked before he thrust her into the bathroom.

'Ask him some questions,' he returned grimly. 'When you come down I'll have a hot drink ready for

you. What the devil's the matter?' he added as she
gave a despairing little screech.

'My soup!' wailed Elinor.

'It's probably burned.'

'There was no smell of burning,' he assured her.

'Don't worry. Denzil probably dealt with it. I'm
sure he'll have saved your precious soup.'

'While you saved my bacon,' she said, managing a
smile at last.

'On the contrary—you saved your own!' He held
her close for a moment, then tousled her bedraggled
hair and left, with terse instructions to get herself
warm and dry as quickly as possible.

The only drawback to this plan was an oversight
on Major Carew's part, thought Elinor wryly. There
was no hot water left in the system after a day without
electricity, courtesy of Alexander Reid. She stripped
off her sodden cloths and left them in the bath, then
washed herself from head to foot, shivering violently
as she towelled herself mercilessly in an effort to get
warmth back into her bruised, aching body.

Eventually, wearing her yellow wool shirt and brown
cords—the last change of clothes in her bag—she
realised that every sweater she'd brought with her was
now damp. She saw that Miles had left one of his
khaki sweaters over the back of the bedroom chair
and decided to borrow it. She breathed in the aroma
of healthy male appreciatively as she rolled up the
sleeves, philosophical about looking rather ridiculous
in a jersey designed for someone almost a foot taller.

Finally, she pulled on an extra pair of socks, thrust
her cold feet into her old suede loafers, then brushed
her damp hair into some semblance of order and
added a touch of colour to her eyes and mouth. It

wouldn't do for Captain Reid to think he'd scared her half to death. Even if he had.

As she went downstairs she heard a hum in the air, and realised the power was back on. The real electrician had obviously arrived. She went into the kitchen, then stopped dead. The Morgans had gone but Alexander Reid was still there, and, worse still, was no longer tied up.

He rose from his chair as she came in, and Elinor backed away, shooting a horrified glance at Miles as he came to take her hand.

'Don't be frightened, Nell,' he said quickly.

'Reid won't hurt you again, I promise.'

'Miss Gibson, I swear I never intended hurting you in the first place,' said the other man, dull red colour rising in his battered face.

'So why did you threaten me with a knife?' she snapped, suddenly deeply, uncontrollably angry. Knocking Miles's hand away, she stalked up to Alexander Reid and stared up into his face, incensed.

'After what you've put us through these last couple of days I hope you get put behind bars where you belong. Poisoning dogs, threatening a little girl—what kind of a man *are* you?'

'Hey, Elinor,' said Miles quickly, taking her arm. 'Calm down——'

'Calm *down*?' she exploded, turning on him. 'This—this maniac threatens our lives and kidnaps me and you tell me to calm down? I thought you were the one who wanted to kill him.'

'I did,' agreed Miles, and pushed her down into a chair by the window. He handed her a mug of coffee.

'Here, drink this.'

She stared at him malevolently, then turned her gaze on Alexander Reid, who in some indefinable way seemed to have shrunk, altered out of all recognition from the fanatic who'd forced her along the cliff.

'So why don't you want to kill him any more, Miles?'

'He's fully entitled to,' said the other man miserably.

'I'm desperately sorry, Miss Gibson. I should never have involved you. When I saw you go over that cliff I wanted to kill myself.'

'What stopped you?' she said contemptuously.

'That young giant who came at me from behind,' returned Alexander Reid with shame.

'He took me by surprise—then Miles got hold of me and began to hit hell out of me, and I was sure I was dead anyway.'

'If Denzil hadn't fired off his shotgun it could have been a close-run thing,' admitted Miles.

'And there was I, certain someone would come dashing after me, and all the while you were playing war-games on the path with never a thought for me,' said Elinor with sarcasm.

Miles's lips twitched.

'Not exactly, Elinor. Unlike Sandy, I knew damn well you were familiar with every nook and cranny down the cliff.'

'I could still have been killed!' she retorted, then winced.

'As it is I've got bruises everywhere. It's a miracle I didn't break a bone or two.'

'I'll give you some liniment,' he promised.

'I don't *want* any liniment!' She fixed Alexander Reid with a basilisk's glare.

'You terrorise me on the phone, cut off my electricity supply, then threaten me with a knife and kidnap me. At the risk of sounding unreasonable, Captain Reid, I think I deserve an explanation.'

'The Spaniards say revenge is a dish best eaten cold,' said Miles obscurely.

'Sandy's just discovered it's best not eaten at all.'

'Very flowery,' said Elinor cuttingly, 'but not very explanatory.'

Alexander Reid, looking infinitely weary, put a shaking hand on the back of one of the kitchen chairs.

'Miss Gibson, you have my word that I wouldn't have harmed you. I just wanted——'

'To use me as a decoy!' she snapped.

'A pity it went a bit wrong, isn't it?'

'Sit down, Sandy,' ordered Miles.

'While I make coffee you can do some talking. You owe us that.'

Alexander Reid took the chair opposite Elinor and looked at her, remorse in the light eyes she'd earlier found so chilling.

'I retired from the army the same time as Miles. Only unlike Miles I had a wife who revelled in army life. Once I was a civilian she left me.'

'You military men just can't seem to hang on to your women, can you?' said Elinor rudely, still seething because Miles Carew obviously had no intention of sending for the police.

'You have my condolences on your loss,' she added abrasively, glad when she saw him wince, 'but I fail to see why it inspired you to your recent activities, Captain Reid.'

'Sandy, please,' he muttered, his eyes falling.

'I doubt we'll ever be on first-name terms,' she snapped, and gave Miles a fulminating look as he brought a tray of coffee to the table.

'You asked for reasons,' said Miles quellingly.

'So keep quiet and listen while Sandy explains.'

Half of her wanted to jump up, collect her belongings and storm back to Cliff Cottage, but curiosity got the better of her. She needed to know why Alexander Reid had set out to terrorise a friend and fellow officer. Heaven help the man's enemies, she thought bitterly.

'You've known Miles all your life, I gather,' began Alexander Reid, after drinking down his coffee gratefully.

'It may help you understand.'

'I doubt it,' said Elinor scornfully.

'Putting a child in danger, not to mention trying to poison the dog...'

'The meat wouldn't have killed, only made it ill,' said the man swiftly, 'and I swear to God I didn't know at first that Sophie was here. Miles was my target. I wanted the dog out of the way, I admit, but a couple of days at the vet's was my aim, nothing worse.'

'Why was Miles your target?' demanded Elinor.

Miles put a hard hand on hers.

'Listen and perhaps we'll find out. I'd heard Sandy was ill, it's true——'

'He means,' Alexander Reid interrupted with dignity, 'that I had a nervous breakdown. When I eventually recovered I was advised to take a holiday somewhere quiet. I chose Tintern. I used to go there as a boy with my parents—fishing, walking and so on. I thought a return to a place I'd liked as a child was a good idea. My sister arranged to come down from Scotland to join me, but she's been held up in the snow. She wants me to go back to Islay with her.

'Anyway, to fill in time until she came, while the weather was still reasonable, I went to Chepstow races. I caught sight of Miles.' His face twisted.

'And suddenly some *alter ego* seemed to take over. I saw Miles as the reason for every ill. We were at Sandhurst at the same time, but I went straight from school; he was an Oxford graduate with a degree...'

He gave Elinor a weary smile.

'You may well look surprised. I'm actually three years younger than Miles. Perhaps we could start my list of black marks against him with that. Then he won the Sword of Honour, and brought the most beautiful girl to the passing-out ball. We both went into the Royal Green Jackets, but his rise was meteoric; mine was pedestrian. He was decorated for his efforts in the Gulf War, I was not. And so that day at the races I went temporarily insane, I suppose— saw him as the reason for everything that had gone wrong in my life.'

'Hell, Sandy,' interjected Miles, thunderstruck.

'Why?'

'God knows.' The other man gave a smile which turned Elinor cold.

'But the blackest mark of all against Miles was chalked up a few years ago when our commanding officer recommended us both for Special Forces application. Both of us managed to survive five weeks of the masochism known as the SAS ''aptitude course'', slogging over the Brecon Beacons with heavy packs, in filthy weather and so on.'

Both he and Miles passed the physical endurance test, he went on to explain, but then had to submit themselves to the daunting final selection, known as 'first sight', their introduction to what the SAS termed 'the Regiment'. Every Special Forces man was present, from the director to the soldiers themselves, and each officer was required to stand up and address the assembled company and convince every man there that he was fit to command. Under the particular democratic system of the Regiment each soldier had a vote.

Miles was accepted, Alexander Reid was not.

'This isn't as bad as it sounds,' said Miles hastily. 'Of the hundred and sixty who went on our particular course, men and officers, only five got through.'

'But you were one of them,' said Alexander Reid bitterly.

'After the nightmare five weeks of pushing myself through the pain barrier, sometimes covering as much as sixty miles in a day loaded down with a bergen heavier than myself, forcing myself to ignore offers of food and warmth, I thought I was home and dry. To be turned down after that was total humiliation— for my wife as well as myself.'

'But that was years ago, Sandy,' said Miles, frowning.

'Why wait until now to get back at me?'

The other man gave a mirthless laugh.

'I didn't realise I wanted to get back at you. I didn't *blame* you, man, I always admired you. But I've been in therapy, trying to get my life back together now I'm out of the army, and I honestly believed I was cured. Then I saw you that day—and something snapped. Some inner demon drove me to show you I was in command at last, the one with the upper hand. But I swear I never meant any real harm.'

Elinor snorted inelegantly.

'Then I hope I'm not around when you do!' She jumped to her feet.

'Right. I'll leave you two old buddies together and go back home. I'll just pop upstairs and collect my wet clothes.'

'Elinor, wait,' said Miles, following her to the kitchen door.

She turned on him fiercely.

'No, I won't wait. Captain Reid's a friend of yours, a fellow officer and *gentleman*, so obviously you don't feel the same animosity towards him as I do. But I've fallen halfway down a cliff, been frightened to death, and somehow, strange as it seems, I have this sudden yearning for peace and quiet safe and sound in my own home now that I'm not afraid to answer the phone any more.'

Alexander Reid stood up, suffering visibly with remorse.

'I'm deeply sorry, Miss Gibson. I wouldn't have done you any physical harm, I swear. I just wanted to get at Miles through you.'

'I can't imagine why,' she said tartly.

'I mean nothing to him; I just happen to live next door.'

Miles's face set in grim lines.

'Nell, I know you've had a terrible fright——'

'*Fright*? I could have been killed!'

'Sandy didn't throw you down the cliff; that was your idea,' he pointed out.

Elinor stared at the two men, plainly united now in fellowship against the unreasonable member of the opposite sex.

'It seemed,' she said with icy dignity, 'like the only course possible at the time. Silly me—I thought my life depended on it. Now I'll get my things and go.'

And nothing Miles could say would deter her. Ten minutes later she left Cliff House, declining escort, and slithered down the drive, then trudged up to Cliff Cottage and let herself in, bolting the door behind her. Turning the newly restored heating up, she filled a kettle, took off Miles's sweater and thrust it with her damp clothes into the washing-machine, made herself a cup of coffee, then sat down on one of the kitchen stools, laid her head on the counter and gave way to a wild storm of tears.

Afterwards she felt a little better—not much, but the bitter knot of resentment in her chest seemed to have loosened a bit. Back there in Cliff House she'd found it hard to breathe for the rage that possessed her when Miles Carew ranged himself on the side of his fellow officer. Men! To blazes with them all: Miles Carew, Alexander Reid and Oliver Maynard included. She made herself a fresh cup of coffee, and this time drank it while it was hot, filled with sudden yearning when she remembered the pan of soup left behind in the kitchen at Cliff House. But the bread crock yielded the half-loaf she'd abandoned when Miles had spirited her away two nights before and now all the drama was over she found, rather to her shame, that she was starving.

Trying hard to forget the soup, she contented herself with toast and marmalade and a couple of chocolate biscuits rather past their first youth, then went upstairs, stripped off her clothes, took the phone off the hook and got into bed, asleep almost the moment her head touched the pillow.

She surfaced to the sound of the doorbell ringing in counterpoint to hammering on the front door. She sat up stiffly in the darkness, her body aching all over as she squinted at her watch. It was seven in the evening, she saw, astonished, and staggered out of bed to pull on her dressing-gown.

'Elinor!' bawled Miles outside in the darkness. 'Are you in there?'

She went downstairs and opened the inner door and then the top half of the outer stable-door.

'Of course I'm here,' she said irritably, glaring at him.

'I was sleeping.'

'Your phone still isn't working,' Miles informed her.

'Yes, it is. I took it off the hook.'

'You did *what*? Didn't it occur to you that I might be worried when there was no answer?' he demanded, incensed.

'No,' she said, yawning.

'I thought you'd be too busy with your chum to worry about me.'

'Don't be childish,' he said curtly.

'Aren't you going to let me in?'

'No, I'm not.'

His eyes narrowed dangerously under the hood of his parka.

'Are you still throwing tantrums about Sandy Reid?'

'*Tantrums*?' She swallowed hard, fought for control but lost, and slammed the half-door in his face, giving a repeat performance with the inner door before ramming the bolts home.

Still incandescent with rage, she limped hurriedly round the house, switching lights on and drawing curtains. She reconnected the telephone then went upstairs and ran a bath full of water as hot as she could stand. Armed with a book, she sank into the water to calm down, vowing to blot Miles Carew—and his friend Alexander Reid—from her mind as she got to grips with a thriller she could enjoy a lot more now the dangers of the last day or two were over.

The phone rang, but she ignored it. Let Miles ring as much as he liked, she wasn't leaving this wonderful womb-like bath until her bruised, battered body felt soothed and her temper was under control again.

Dressed in her father's warm pyjamas, thick socks and her own dressing-gown, she finally emerged from the bathroom feeling a great deal better. She went downstairs and transferred the clothes to her mother's tumble-drier, then took another loaf of bread out of the freezer and put an already defrosted chicken and leek pie in the oven. When the phone rang she eyed it mutinously for a moment, then, with a sigh, took it from the hook and pulled out the aerial.

'All right, all right, Miles,' she said wearily.

'I'm sorry I——'

'Who the hell is Miles?' demanded an irate voice, and Elinor bit her lip.

'Oliver? How did you know I was here?'

'One doesn't have to be Sherlock Holmes to conclude you'd run for cover to Stavely. Your friend Linda was suitably mysterious about your whereabouts, I hasten to add, so no necessity to chastise her.'

'Why are you ringing, Oliver?' she asked without warmth.

'You can't imagine I intended to leave things as they were!'

'Why not? I said everything I needed to say the other night.'

'I, however, did not. Would it be overstepping the bounds of intimacy to enquire where you've been the last couple of days? I've tried contacting you several times, but up to now with no success.'

'The phone was out of order for a while. Have you tried tonight? Before now, I mean?'

'No. I've only just got in. Some of us,' added Oliver silkily, 'had work to do at the office.'

So it must have been Miles earlier on. Elinor felt a little glow of pleasure.

'Which reminds me, Oliver,' she said quickly.

'Please accept my resignation.'

'Certainly not, I don't accept anything,' he retorted, 'neither my *congé*, Elinor, nor your resignation. I assume you've been held up by snow in your country retreat. As soon as it clears I want you back here and all this nonsense put behind us.'

'No chance, on either count,' she said succinctly, and put the phone down.

When it rang again a minute or two later she abandoned her inspection of the pie in the oven and snatched up the phone.

'Look here, Oliver——'

'Miles, actually,' said a wry, dry voice.

'Problems, Nell?'

After Oliver's indulgent, self-confident tone Miles's voice seemed doubly attractive. Not, thought Elinor, that she was about to let him know that.

'Nothing I can't handle,' she assured him shortly.

'I've no doubt of that, Elinor! I'm sure you're equal to anything—I could have done with you in the Gulf.'

'Talking of which,' she said tartly, 'is your friend still with you?'

'No. I came down to tell you that earlier and got a door in my face for my pains.'

'That was childish of me. I apologise—for the door, anyway.'

'But you're still angry with me for failing to clap Sandy in irons.'

'Frankly, yes.'

'He's got such a lot on his plate I didn't feel I could add to it. His marriage is washed up, and his illness has put paid to the job he had lined up.'

'For which I have sympathy. I still don't see why he had to turn on you—and on me, while he was at it, not to mention Sophie and the dog.'

'I'm not condoning his behaviour. But in a way I can understand it. If my life was in ruins and I couldn't see Sophie I'd probably break up too.'

'I doubt that very much. Anyway, where is he now?'

'Back at his hotel in Tintern. Tomorrow his sister arrives. She's older than Sandy, widow of a colonel of the Royal Scots Dragoon Guards. There's not much that Elspeth Muir doesn't know about army life and the withdrawal symptoms of those who leave it.' Miles paused.

'Do you still want revenge, Elinor?'

'I suppose not. Captain Reid didn't find it sweet, so I don't imagine I would either.'

'But it still rankles that I no longer wanted to kill him once the drama was over.'

'Yes,' she said candidly.

'I'm obviously built of more ignoble clay than you, Miles.'

He laughed.

'I seriously doubt that. It's just that I could understand what was happening to Sandy, that's all. In some measure I feel sorry for him. While you, my little Amazon, rouse rather different feelings on my part.'

'Well I felt sorry for me,' she retorted, rather flushed.

'I never got any of that soup!'

'You would have if you'd opened your door—I brought some down for you.' Miles paused.

'Does this mean you've got nothing to eat? I found some chops in the kitchen, by the way. What do I do with them?'

'Grill them, then eat them.'

'On my own?'

'Afraid so. I've organised my dinner. I'm heating one of Mother's famed chicken pies as we speak.'

'What a self-sufficient creature! By the way, am I allowed to ask why your Oliver rang?'

'He seems to think I should go back and take up where we left off before the break-up. Both relationships, professional and private. I'm to put all this nonsense behind me, I think was the phrase.'

'Brave man,' said Miles with respect.

'But then he was on the other end of a telephone line. Would he have dared say that to your face?'

Elinor let out an unwilling chuckle.

'Oh, probably. Oliver's very—well, sure of himself.'

'Is he right to be sure?'

'If you mean am I going to do as he wants, no, I'm not.'

'And does your deep disapproval of my leniency extend to the job I offered?'

'Jobs are too hard to come by to cut my nose off to spite my face,' Elinor assured him briskly.

'If you still want me to work for you, I will.'

He gave a wry laugh.

'Then we'll take it as settled. By the way,' he added, 'I had a word with Sophie tonight. She's had enough of puppy-sitting. The forecast's good for tomorrow— do you fancy a trip to Ludlow to fetch her? The roads should be all right in the Range Rover.'

'Will there be room?'

'The Hedleys went in their own car. They'll drive back separately.'

Elinor thought about it, wondering if it seemed a bit spineless to capitulate so easily. But now she'd had time to recover she felt better disposed towards Miles than she'd have thought possible earlier—especially after the exchange with Oliver. Odd how she'd never realised what a pompous voice he had. And a drive to Ludlow with Miles sounded like a far better proposition than a day on her own at the cottage without transport.

'All right, then, yes, I'd like to.'

'Good. Tennish? We can have lunch there and get back here before dark.'

'Right. I'd better get cracking on some ironing after supper so I can look respectable for the trip. I washed your sweater,' she added.

'That's very kind of you, though quite unnecessary. I would have preferred it fragrant from contact with you, Elinor.'

She coloured brilliantly, glad he couldn't see.

'At the time I was so furious with you—and men in general—I just slung it in the machine with everything else.'

'Are you more reconciled to me—and my sex—by now?'

'More or less.' She laughed suddenly.

'Unless Oliver starts getting bombastic again.'

'You could always refer him to me if he becomes troublesome,' suggested Miles crisply.

'I mean it, Elinor. After all, I've known you since you were a baby. In your father's absence who better to fight your battles?'

'I fight my own battles, thanks just the same.'

'So I noticed,' he said drily.

'Goodnight, Elinor. Lock your door carefully, please.'

'I already have. I made sure you heard me!' she returned, laughing.

'And I'm bloody determined you won't do that to me again, too,' he returned, a note in his voice that lingered with her long after he'd rung off.

CHAPTER SIX

MILES arrived at Cliff Cottage at a little after nine next morning. Elinor let him in, surprised, and ushered him into the kitchen.

'I thought you said ten,' she remarked, waving to a chair at the table. 'I've just made tea. Would you like some?'

'Yes, please.' Miles sat in the rush-seated chair, stretching his long legs out in front of him. 'I was up early, so I thought I'd come and make my peace with you before we set out.'

'You did that on the phone last night,' she pointed out. 'Want something to eat? No eggs, but I can do you a nice line in toast and marmalade.'

He grinned. 'Thanks. I accept. I'd got rather used to breakfasting with you—dining with you too. I was lonely on my own last night.'

She frowned as she put four more slices of bread in the toaster. 'Until a short time ago you'd forgotten I existed, so cut the soft soap, please.'

'No soft soap about it,' he retorted, his eyes following her as she collected another cup and saucer and pushed butter and marmalade towards him. 'Our recent crisis revived our acquaintance pretty rapidly. Besides, I've known you, on and off, all your life, remember. Though when you catapulted into my life again it was quite a shock to find the androgynous little urchin metamorphosed into a beautiful, unmistakably feminine woman.'

96

Elinor thrust slices of toast into a white pottery rack and handed it to him, frowning. 'It's too early in the morning for this type of conversation.'

He met her eyes with a look which brought quick, glowing colour to her newly washed face. 'Then choose whatever time suits you better to resume it.'

'Always assuming I wish to,' she retorted, busying herself with the teapot.

'Are you still angry with me about Sandy?'

'No. Now I've calmed down I feel sorry for him, I suppose. Though why he had to terrorise us like that I still find hard to understand.'

'So do I, in one way. But in another I suppose I can see how he regarded himself as a failure and me as a success, both in my career and with women.'

'But you were divorced.'

'Ah, yes, but then you arrived on the scene, yet another beautiful woman in my life, and that, he told me, was when everything went completely haywire.' He held out his teacup for a refill. 'Until he saw you he was content with having disrupted my life a bit, got rid of the dog, made me send Sophie and the Hedleys away. He swears he was satisfied, that he'd have gone back to the hotel, rung me to gloat over me just before he took off for Scotland, and that would have been that. Then he saw you with me, assumed we were lovers and his plan of campaign took an ugly U-turn.'

'Is that when he started the phone calls and cut off the electricity and so on?'

'Right.'

'So what did he expect to achieve by kidnapping me?'

'You were exactly what he said—a decoy to get me out in the open.' Miles shrugged. 'He suddenly needed to confront me face to face.'

'I still don't get it,' said Elinor flatly. 'All right, so supposing I hadn't dived over the cliff and I was still his prisoner when you came charging after us. What was to have happened then?'

'Sandy just meant to keep you captive in the lookout. When I arrived on cue he planned to dangle you over the balustrade, demonstrating that at last this was one situation where I was helpless and he was in complete control. Once I'd admitted that it would have been all over.'

'That's sick! You honestly believe that?' said Elinor scornfully.

'I'll never know if I do or not,' returned Miles, disposing of the last piece of toast. 'You gave Sandy the shock of his life by falling over the cliff, at which point Chris Morgan appears to his rear, I attack him from the front and start hitting hell out of him, Denzil fires off his gun and Captain Alexander Reid breaks down and cries like a baby.'

'Oh, I *see*. That's why you were so sorry for him,' said Elinor, enlightened.

'It wasn't the tears, so much as his shame for shedding them,' said Miles soberly. 'At that point I just left him to the Morgans and went down over the cliff after you.'

'What if I hadn't been in the Hide?' she asked curiously. 'What if I really had fallen down the cliff?'

He breathed in deeply, got up and pulled her to her feet. 'That,' he said grimly, 'is something that kept me awake most of last night, why I'm up so early this morning, and why I couldn't eat any breakfast until

I'd seen you again to make sure you were really in one piece. One very delectable piece,' he added, his voice deepening, and jerked her close and kissed her hard.

After a moment he raised his head and stared into her startled eyes. 'And don't tell me it's too early for this too, because it's not.' He kissed her again and went on kissing her until Elinor forgot the time, the day and everything else other than the hard, obliterating kisses, and clever, importuning hands which found responsive nerve-ends right through several layers of clothes.

She kissed him back, surrendering to his conquering tongue, any last shreds of animosity vanishing so quickly that it soon became glaringly obvious that if she didn't call a halt immediately she wouldn't be able to at all. And neither would Miles.

With a superhuman effort she thrust him away and dodged round the table, panting, her colour high and her eyes glittering.

'We're supposed to be on our way to collect your daughter,' she gasped with difficulty, and Miles breathed in deeply, his hands clenched, white-knuckled, on the back of a kitchen chair.

'I wish we weren't,' he said with brutal honesty. 'I want nothing more in the world than to take you to bed right now, Nell.'

She glared at him. 'And you think I'd agree, just like that?'

He shook his head. 'No. I'm just telling you exactly how I feel. I think, I hope you feel at least something of the same, but I can't be sure. Women, in my experience at least, don't function in the same way as men.'

'I'm not "women", Miles,' she said acidly. 'I'm me. With my own set of rules to play by.'

'If you tell me what they are I'll do my best to play by them too,' he informed her, in command of himself again.

Elinor looked at him narrowly. 'You mean that?'

His mouth took on a rueful twist. 'I'll probably live to regret it, but yes, I mean it.'

'First of all, if we're going to work together it's not a good idea to get physically involved.'

'You managed it with this Oliver of yours.'

'And look where that got me! Besides, with him it was different...' She halted, flushing, and his eyes hardened.

'You mean because you were in love with him?'

Elinor gazed up at him, biting her lip. 'No. I know now I was never in love with Oliver—something I should have realised sooner and saved a lot of trouble.'

'So what's the problem?'

Was this the point where she did without honesty and fudged her reasons? Or did she tell the truth and hope Miles wouldn't misunderstand?

'It must be perfectly obvious,' Elinor began stiffly, 'that when you kiss me I—well—I mean we...'

'Go up in flames?' offered Miles helpfully.

She bit her lip, flushing. 'It's not like that for me usually. With other men, I mean.'

The dark eyes narrowed to a triumphant gleam. 'Including Oliver?'

Elinor nodded reluctantly.

'Of course,' said Miles silkily, 'the reason could be a lot simpler than that—something to do with those basic impulses I once boasted were not a ruling factor in my life. I was wrong, Elinor. At this moment I'm having trouble keeping my hands off you.'

'In which case,' she said, above the thumping of her heart, 'I think working together is a bad idea.'

Miles eyed her in silence for some time. 'Even if I promise never to touch you—unless invited?'

'Would you keep to that?'

'I could try,' he said honestly. 'But after yesterday it's difficult.'

'Why yesterday?'

'Because when I thought you'd fallen down the cliff I felt as though part of me had gone with you.' The dark eyes locked with hers. 'Don't get me wrong, Elinor. I'm not saying I suddenly realised I was in love with you, because I've been through all that nonsense with Selina. The gut-wrenching feeling I had staring down that cliff wasn't the same thing at all.'

'It was like your reaction when Sophie was threatened,' she suggested hastily. 'I was your responsibility and it went wrong.'

Miles smiled wryly. 'I don't think of you as a responsibility, or as a daughter—as I demonstrated just now. I just know I want you in my life in whatever capacity you agree to. If it's only as my secretary I'll settle for that—for now at least,' he added, eyes glinting. 'But I'd be lying if I said I didn't want more than that. I've enjoyed having you with me these past few days. I like having you around. Do your rules allow you to work for a man who wants you as a friend and companion too?'

Elinor looked at him, trying hard for detachment. To hear Miles Carew telling her he wanted her in his life in some way was the realisation of a dream she'd thought she'd stopped dreaming years ago. 'I think,' she began carefully, 'that we've been living on our nerves for the past day or two. I suggest we fetch Sophie and spend time with her, and I'll give you a hand with some of your more immediate paperwork for the project. After a while I'll go back to Cheltenham and sort things out there, and in a couple of weeks, if you feel like bringing the subject up again, I'll listen.'

He looked at her without expression. 'And Oliver?'

'Oliver's no longer part of my life,' she returned positively. 'But I have to get back to make that clear to him, even work out my notice with his firm if he insists on it.'

'You'll tell him you've got another job?'

She gave him a long, steady look, then smiled suddenly, her eyes dancing. 'Yes, I will. After all, it doesn't matter how angry he gets, does it? My new employer won't insist on a reference!'

The drive to Ludlow, despite the rapid thaw, took longer than expected. Sophie Carew was in a fever of impatience by the time her father arrived at the Miller's Arms for lunch. As the Range Rover parked outside the inn she came dashing out, a slim, dark-haired child in scarlet sweater and jeans, so much a miniature version of her father that Elinor smiled at him in amusement.

'A chip off the old block.'

Miles grinned and jumped down to swing his small daughter off her feet. He gave her poppy-red cheek a smacking kiss as he listened to her non-stop account of her stay at the inn and Daisy and the puppies, and her stern recriminations because he hadn't brought Meg along to fetch her.

'She's still at the kennels, chatterbox,' he said, chuckling, and held up a hand to help Elinor down. 'I brought someone else along instead. This is Elinor, Dr Gibson's daughter from next door.'

Sophie looked surprised for a moment, her narrow dark face questioning, then she flipped her braid over her shoulder and took the hand Elinor held out. 'Hello. I know your mummy.'

'So I've heard,' returned Elinor, smiling, and squeezed the small hand. 'She's told me a lot about you, Sophie. I'm very pleased to meet you at last.'

Sophie returned the smile politely, obviously battling to hide her disappointment at not having her father to herself.

'Mrs Hedley's helping make a special lunch, and Hedley's in bed with flu,' she told him importantly. 'You're to come straight to the dining-room 'cos lunch is nearly ready.'

Miles exchanged a look with Elinor as they went through the low door of the inn. 'Mrs H said nothing about Tom's flu when I talked with her last night.'

'Maybe it's come on overnight.'

When Mrs Hedley came to greet them it was plain she was flustered. 'Hello, Mr Miles—why, Elinor, what a surprise; how nice to see you. What with the doctor coming and everything, I'm sorry, but we're a bit behind with the meal.'

'Never mind that, Mrs H—what's up with Tom?'

Tom Hedley, it transpired, had been feeling seedy for a day or two, but wouldn't admit it.

'You know how obstinate he is,' said his wife, looking worried. 'Terrible temperature he's got, and he doesn't look too clever at all. I was that worried because of Sophie catching it.'

'Then don't worry any more,' said Miles at once. He put an arm around his small daughter. 'After lunch we'll take her home out of the way, and you can stay and look after Tom until he's fighting fit again.'

'But I can't do that,' protested Mrs Hedley in distress. 'Who's going to look after you?'

Elinor recognised a cue when she heard one. 'Actually I've got some time off and nothing to do with it,' she said cheerfully. 'If Miles and Sophie are brave enough to chance my cooking I'll be happy to help out until you get back.'

'Thank you, Elinor,' said Miles quickly, before Mrs Hedley could say a word. 'We accept with pleasure— don't we, Sophie?'

Sophie, plainly not terribly thrilled at the new arrangement, nodded without enthusiasm. 'When will you come back, Mrs Hedley?' she asked, looking worried.

'As soon as possible, never you fret,' said the other woman, who, having known Elinor best as a tomboy who wheedled cakes out of her with Harry and Mark, obviously had little faith in her domestic talents.

'Don't worry,' said Elinor reassuringly. 'I really can cook, you know. Mother saw to that.'

Mrs Hedley's face cleared a little at the mention of Dr Mary Gibson; she asked after both Elinor's parents, then went to fetch her sister Beryl to be introduced.

After a simple, superbly cooked lunch of soup and roast beef, followed by a treacle tart served with Beryl's own wonderful vanilla ice-cream, or in Miles's case a wedge of Stilton eaten with home-made oatcakes, it was decided that Miles, Elinor and Sophie should make a start for Stavely while the weather held up.

'Come and see Daisy's babies first,' urged Sophie.

In the barn behind the inn a black labrador of great charm was holding court with her young. With an exclamation of pleasure Elinor went down on her knees beside the great basket full of wriggling black-satin puppies, careful to ask Daisy's permission to stroke the plump, heaving little bodies.

'Aren't they gorgeous?' she exclaimed to Sophie, and the child nodded, pleased, then heaved a downcast sigh.

'What is it, darling?' asked Miles.

'Mrs Dodd says Daisy can't keep them all. People have bought some of them already. Can't we have one, Daddy?'

'But we've got Meg,' he reminded her.

Elinor saw the bright dark eyes fill with tears, and to her own dismay heard herself blurt, 'I could have one, Sophie.'

Her eyes met Miles's defiantly.

'It could complicate your life,' he pointed out.

But Sophie was looking at Elinor with wet, grateful eyes. 'Will you? Really? I'll help you look after her.'

'Her?' said Miles.

Sophie nodded vigorously, pointing out one of the yelping black puppies. 'That's the one I like best.'

To Elinor they all looked exactly the same. But she loved dogs, and there'd always been one in residence at Cliff Cottage until recently. At which point it dawned on her that her home would soon belong to Miles, not her parents.

'Her name's Jet,' said Sophie in a small voice, sensing indecision in Elinor.

'Good name,' approved Elinor, vanquished by the appeal in Sophie's eyes.

'We'll always have her if you're obliged to go away for a day or two,' said Miles, looking, to Elinor at least, distinctly smug.

'Then that's settled,' she said, convinced she'd taken leave of her senses. She jumped to her feet, brushing the knees of her jeans. 'I'll go and ask Mrs Dodd how much she wants for Jet.'

'Allow me to make you a present of her,' said Miles quickly. 'Since you've so nobly stepped into the breach to take care of us it's the least I can do.'

She protested at first, but when she discovered exactly how much a pedigree labrador puppy cost she was forced to take advantage of Miles's offer, and shortly afterwards they were on their way back to Stavely complete with collar, lead, feeding-bowls, a basket for Jet's bed and a supply of puppy food. Jet wasn't at all happy being parted from her mother, nor at travelling in the Range Rover, and Sophie was fully occupied for most of the journey in quieting the shrieking puppy—and telling Jet how much she was going to like living in Stavely, and how next day there would be a lovely big dog to play with and lots of space to run in the garden, and on and on in a soothing mantra that eventually had the desired effect and put both the puppy and herself to sleep.

'Having qualms?' said Miles, lips twitching.

Elinor glanced over at the sleeping passengers in the back seat. 'Too true I am,' she said in an undertone. 'I thought recent events would have cured me of acting on impulse. But here I am again, jumping in with both feet because I just couldn't resist the look in your daughter's eyes.'

'I only wish her father's had the same effect,' he murmured.

Elinor sent him a glittering, sidelong glance. 'Even if they did, from now on I'm not succumbing to it. Between cooking and coping with the hound back there, not to mention trying to ingratiate myself with Sophie, I imagine life will be complicated enough.'

'I wonder,' said Miles thoughtfully, 'why you feel you must ingratiate yourself with Sophie?'

Elinor cursed the tide of colour which flooded her face. 'If I'm going to work with you,' she said with dignity, 'it seems only wise to make friends with your daughter. You suggested it, remember, asked me to visit her while she's in this transition period before she makes friends locally.'

'So I did. Thank you, Elinor.'

She fell silent, knowing perfectly well that her reasons for making friends with Sophie were a little more complicated than just wanting a good relationship with the child of a prospective employer. She wanted Sophie to like her because Sophie was Miles Carew's daughter, it was true, but there was more to it than that. Sophie was an attractive, lovable child, but the hint of wariness in her eyes cut Elinor to the heart.

Selina Carew had a lot to answer for, she thought, remembering her own carefree, secure childhood. She reminded herself that it was pointless to condemn Selina without knowing the entire story. Nevertheless Elinor felt certain that nothing in the world would make her give up any child she produced, and certainly not just for marriage to a rich man unwilling to take on the role of stepfather.

'That's a very fierce expression,' commented Miles, glancing at her. 'A penny for them, Elinor?'

She heaved a sigh. 'Since you've already paid a fortune for the hound back there you can have my thoughts for free. I'm worried I've bitten off more than I can chew.'

'You think your parents will object to the introduction of Jet into Cliff Cottage?'

Elinor stared at him in horror. 'I hadn't even thought of that! I was too much taken up in how I was going to manage. I never gave a thought to Mother and Dad.'

Miles grinned as they turned up the winding drive to Cliff House. 'By the time they return Jet will be a model of obedience, and they'll be too taken up with the move to Monmouth to worry about dogs. Besides,' he added, 'the new owner won't cut up rough about a few teeth-marks in the woodwork.'

Elinor groaned as they drew up in front of the coach-house. 'I forgot puppies chew things. I'll have to roll up all Mother's precious rugs . . .'

'For the time being Jet's home will be Cliff House,' said Miles with emphasis. 'I'd like you to live in until the Hedleys get back.'

Elinor stared at him. 'Oh, but——'

'You'd be doing me a great favour,' he broke in. 'Sophie's used to having someone in the house all the time. With the new arrangements for the property afoot I need to be out a lot. Having you on hand would be a godsend, Nell.'

She thought it over. 'Look, Miles, I'll gladly stay on hand all day until Sophie goes to bed, but I'd rather sleep at Cliff Cottage.'

His face hardened. 'Why? Are you afraid I'll walk in my sleep? With Sophie under the same roof?'

'It never crossed my mind,' she said hotly. 'I just want to sleep in my own bed while Cliff Cottage is still my home, that's all. I've lived there all my life, remember. Moving out's going to be a wrench.'

He relaxed a little. 'Of course. Sorry. Sophie and I will be grateful for whatever time you can spare. I realise I've complicated your life, Elinor.' His mouth twisted. 'Are you sorry you came running home that night?'

'If I'd known what I was getting myself into, one way and another, I'd have been wiser to stay put in Cheltenham.'

Miles switched off the ignition and turned to her. 'Would you prefer to put the clock back and restore your relationship with Oliver?'

Their eyes met and held, then Elinor shook her head slowly.

'No.'

'Who's Oliver?' demanded a sleepy voice from the back. 'Oh, dear! *Daddy*—Jet needs to go walkies!'

Instantly everyone was galvanised into action. Miles lifted Sophie down and Elinor clipped the lead to the puppy's collar and all three of them went with Jet on her first inspection of the garden. It was lit up already in the gathering dusk, the security beams pouring light over the gleaming white lawns and hedges, showing that the thaw had done little this high up on the cliff's edge.

'I ought to go home first,' said Elinor, 'and see if everything's all right at the cottage.'

'We'll come with you,' Miles said firmly. 'Sophie, keep a firm grip on that lead once we're indoors, we'll keep Jet in the kitchen while Elinor has a look round.'

'But Daddy,' complained Sophie, once they'd installed the puppy's equipment in the kitchen at Cliff Cottage, 'she'll be ever so lonely in here on her own tonight. She'll miss her mummy.'

Something in the child's voice pierced Elinor to the heart. The look Miles exchanged with her told her he felt the same.

'If she does I'll get up in the night and cuddle her,' she said firmly to Sophie and the child's eyes lit up.

'Will you? Truly?'

'On my honour, cross my heart,' Elinor assured her. 'But in the day you'll have to introduce her to Meg and get them used to each other.'

'Course I will.' Sophie smiled seraphically at her father. 'We're lucky El—Elinor can come and look after us now Mrs Hedley can't, aren't we?'

'Very lucky indeed,' said Miles, looking Elinor in the eye. He bent to put a bowl of water down for the puppy. 'Now make sure you keep this filled, Nell. If it's some time since you had a dog perhaps you'll have forgotten how thirsty they get.'

'Right,' she said.

'Daddy called you *Nell*,' remarked Sophie. 'Can I do that too, please?'

Elinor gave her a sudden hug. 'By all means, Sophie Carew.'

Obviously encouraged, the child gave her a cajoling look. 'Can you cook burgers? Mrs Hedley says she doesn't hold with them.'

CHAPTER SEVEN

CLIFF HOUSE had been built at the turn of the century, with large, spacious rooms, and a sufficiency of servants to keep them all immaculate, including four gardeners for the extensive grounds which surrounded the house. Now, with even the Hedleys' services unavailable, the doors were closed firmly on all rooms other than the kitchen, the study, and the bedrooms and bathrooms in use for Sophie and Miles.

'Fortunately the snow hides any deficiencies in the garden,' he said wryly, once he was alone with Elinor after dinner, Jet curled up asleep in front of the study fire. Sophie had needed promises of burgers and beans and ice-cream next day, and any other lures Miles could throw out, before she could be coaxed to leave the puppy downstairs and settle down for the night with only his old teddy for company.

'Mrs Hedley obviously doesn't approve of convenience foods,' said Elinor, amused.

'Absolutely not. She'd do anything else in the world for Sophie, but fresh, nourishing home-cooking is the order of the day under her regime. The nearest to fast food she allows is ice-cream!' Miles's face set. 'Selina obviously placed no such restrictions on her daughter's diet.'

'It hasn't done Sophie any harm,' said Elinor, striving to be fair. 'A healthier-looking child would be hard to find. Those rosy cheeks are irresistible.'

'Her colour isn't normally so high. Must be the warmth in the house after running about in the snow.'

'Mm,' said Elinor, stretching. 'After a couple of days without heating this is wonderful—we could do without the fire really, though I do love watching the flames.'

'A pity, then, that you're obliged to go out into the freezing night and leave them,' Miles pointed out drily. 'Why won't you stay for just a couple of nights at least, Nell?'

'Because there's no reason to, and you know it. The danger's over.' To hide how much she longed to stay Elinor jumped to her feet. 'Right. Jet here needs a walk, and the stroll home to the cottage will fill the bill nicely.'

'With Sophie asleep upstairs I can't even come with you,' objected Miles bitterly, helping her into her jacket.

Elinor chuckled. 'Nothing can happen to me between here and the cottage, Miles. I've got a guard dog now, remember.'

He eyed the dozing puppy. 'I can't say that reassures me much. Promise you'll ring if you change your mind. Or if you want me,' he added huskily, looking at her suddenly.

The unguarded look in her eyes told him without words exactly how much she wanted him. He held out his arms and she walked into them, holding up her mouth, yielding exultantly when Miles caught her in a rib-cracking embrace. He thrust aside her coat to slide long, caressing fingers over the wool covering her breasts as he kissed her with a hungry intensity which made her senses reel. With superhuman effort she pulled away at last, helped by the puppy, who'd woken up and wanted to join in.

'I do want you,' she said, breathing rapidly. 'Something which must be perfectly obvious. It's not a feeling I'm familiar with, and it's making me nervous.'

His eyes blazed under lowered lids. 'But I thought you and Oliver were lovers.'

'I thought so too, but we weren't in the true sense of the word.'

'What do you mean?'

'I think you know exactly what I mean.' Elinor thrust a hand through her tumbled hair. 'Oliver shared my bed—I shared his too—on several occasions. It was pleasant enough—he's no callow, impatient teenager. But all the enthusiasm for the arrangement was on his side.'

'Then why the hell did you agree to it?'

'Because I thought I was in love with him, I was going to marry him and I knew it was expected of me. I wouldn't even admit to myself that I was a bit disappointed. I thought things would improve with—with practice.'

'But they didn't.'

'No. But perhaps I didn't give it enough time...'

'How much time did it take the first time we exchanged even one kiss?' he said triumphantly. 'If the fire's there it ignites, Elinor. If it doesn't it never will.'

She heaved a deep, shaky breath, then bent to clip the leash to the puppy's collar. 'I realised that eventually.' She straightened, smiling coaxingly into Miles's set face. 'Anyway, it seems best that I go home to sleep. Otherwise *I* might be the one guilty of sleep-walking.'

His face softened. 'A seductive thought, Nell. I'll try to dream about it.'

'A good night's sleep would be better—for both of us,' she said, smiling, and led the puppy towards the door. 'I'll arrive about eight to cook breakfast.'

'You needn't,' he assured her. 'I'm perfectly capable of managing that myself. Why not have a lie-in tomorrow?'

Elinor grinned down at the bouncing puppy. 'Some hopes! I rather fancy my alarm clock here will have me up at the crack of dawn.'

Miles went upstairs to check on a sleeping Sophie, then walked with Elinor as far as the drive to the cottage before parting with her, giving her strict instructions to ring him once she was settled for the night.

'I'm only next door,' she said practically. 'And Captain Reid is now safe with his sister, so I'll be fine. No more nasty phone calls!'

On the last Elinor was wrong. The moment she was through the door the telephone rang. Hurrying past the extension in the hall, she went into the kitchen with Jet, closed the door and picked up the receiver from the wall phone.

'Elinor? Where the hell have you been?' demanded Oliver, in tones that would have alienated her even if their relationship had still been on its old footing.

'To Ludlow, actually,' she said coolly. 'Why? Did you want something, Oliver?'

'What the hell were you doing driving to Ludlow in weather like this?'

'I wasn't driving myself. And, Oliver,' she went on with emphasis, 'I thought I made it clear the other night that from now on what I do and where I go is entirely my own concern. I gave you back your ring, and I'm finishing with the firm. I'm sorry, Oliver. We would never have suited.'

'Just because I don't happen to enjoy the company of your immature circle of friends?' he demanded cuttingly.

'That was part of it, yes.'

'Am I allowed to ask the nature of your other objections?'

'I'd rather you didn't—oh, no!' she broke off.

'What's the matter?'

'I'll have to ring off; my new puppy's just puddled on the kitchen floor.'

'*Puppy*? I thought you liked cats?'

'No, Oliver, you're the one who likes cats. I like dogs. I'll come into the office as soon as I can to collect my things.'

There was a pause. 'Won't you at least work a month's notice?' he asked bleakly.

'Under the circumstances that would be awkward for both of us—and everyone else at the firm. I'm perfectly happy to forgo any salary owing,' she added.

'Surely you know me better than that?' he said bitterly. 'Do I take it you've already found another job?'

'Yes, or rather the job found me—— Look, I really must ring off; the puppy's added insult to injury on the floor. Goodbye, Oliver.'

After Elinor had mopped up the puppy's transgressions and given her a small quantity of milk to drink, the telephone rang again. This time it was her flatmate, Linda, demanding details of Elinor's activities and when she intended coming back. After a brief résumé of her future plans, which included a visit to the flat to collect some badly needed clothes, Elinor assured

Linda that her new man could stay as long as he liked for the time being, but warned her not to make the arrangement permanent.

'I'll need my bolt-hole to come back to some time,' she explained. 'Tell you more when I see you.'

Finally, just as Elinor was in her dressing-gown and trying to persuade Jet to sleep in the kitchen, Miles rang.

'Everything all right?'

'Fine. Jet has problems with staying in her bed alone, but I'm sure I'll get it through to her eventually.'

'I rang earlier. The line was busy.'

'My flatmate, Linda,' said Elinor, wondering why she felt it necessary to explain. 'Oliver too,' she added reluctantly.

'Demanding your return?'

'In a way. But I think he got the message. Finally.'

'Poor chap,' said Miles, with such obvious insincerity that Elinor giggled.

'You couldn't care less!'

'True. And I've told you before—if he gets troublesome refer him to me. I'm an old family friend, remember, fully entitled to protect you from all comers.'

'Including yourself?' said Elinor rashly.

'That, I admit, is more of a problem. I keep trying to remind myself that Elinor Gibson was once a grubby little urchin who kept landing my brothers in hot water. I can remember one occasion very vividly. I wanted to spank you hard when I found you stuck in the top of the tallest tree in the grounds. Harry had sprained his ankle trying to rescue you and I was required to get you down to terra firma in one piece.'

'You were horribly efficient about it, and I do mean horrible,' said Elinor with feeling. 'After the lecture you gave me I cried myself to sleep afterwards.'

'Did you?' he asked softly.

'Yes.'

'If you were here with me now I could make amends.'

Elinor cleared her throat. 'When I said the danger was over I was wrong. It's you I should have been worrying about, not Captain Reid!'

'I just want us to be friends, Nell.'

'Do you?'

There was a pause. 'Yes,' he said at last, his voice lower by half an octave. '*Close* friends.'

Elinor would have found it hard to sleep anyway after Miles's parting shot, but even if she'd had any plans for a good night's rest Jet was determined to ruin them. The moment she was left alone in the dark in the kitchen the puppy shrieked so piteously that Elinor went back and turned on the light, hoping this would help.

It failed. Jet objected so ear-piercingly once the kitchen door was shut that Elinor finally gave up. She made a mental apology to her mother, who had strong views about keeping dogs downstairs, and took Jet, basket and all, up to her own bedroom and settled her beside the bed.

The puppy sat upright in her blanket-lined nest, eyeing Elinor's every move closely until she was settled in bed, then, the moment the light was off, scrabbled up the quilt and made it very clear that she would sleep on the bed by Elinor or not at all. After a few arguments on the subject Elinor was so weary she gave

in, but after a stern lecture on the subject of puddles.
Jet took these so much to heart that at six o'clock she
was awake and emitting an ear-splitting request to be
let out.

Dazed with sleep, Elinor stumbled downstairs with
the puppy under her arm, let her out into the dark,
snowy garden, then cursed herself for all kinds of fool
when the puppy promptly disappeared from view.
Pulling on rubber boots and a raincoat of her
mother's, Elinor snatched up a torch and rushed into
the garden in her nightgown. Calling for Jet through
chattering teeth, she ran down the drive in time to see
a small black shape making a beeline for Cliff House
and tore after it, activating the security lights. Next
moment the front door opened and Miles shot out in
his dressing-gown.

'Elinor! What's wrong—has someone broken in—
are you all right?'

He caught her in his arms but she shook her head,
struggling to get free. 'Jet!' she gasped. 'She...
ran...away!'

Miles cursed, grabbed the torch, then laughed as a
small black bundle came gambolling up to them, obviously enjoying itself enormously. He scooped up the
puppy and grabbed Elinor by the hand, rushing her
to the front door and into the house.

'You're frozen!' he exclaimed, and took her into
the kitchen, which, by contrast to the temperature
outside, was blissfully warm. He switched on the
heating, eyeing her outfit in amusement. Elinor
hugged her arms round herself, colouring.

'I can't stop,' she said quickly. 'I was in such a rush
to chase after madam here, I left the back door
unlocked. I should have taken her on the lead. Sorry

to make such a commotion, Miles. I hope I didn't wake Sophie.'

'I'll just go and see, then I'll take you back.' He turned at the kitchen door, wagging a finger at her. 'If you'd stayed here as I wanted we could have avoided all this.'

'You wouldn't have enjoyed the operatic objections I had to put up with last night,' said Elinor with feeling. 'Jet flatly refused to sleep anywhere except on my bed.'

Miles grinned. 'I can't say I blame her.'

Elinor let out an unwilling chuckle as he went off to check on Sophie, and leaned on one of the rapidly heating radiators while she cuddled the puppy, which was now fast asleep in her arms. What had she taken on? she thought, sighing. And not only with the puppy, either. Sophie needed lots of cuddling too, unless she was much mistaken, while Miles's requirements were something it didn't do to dwell on.

'That's a very stern face,' he said, coming back into the room, carrying a tartan wool blanket. 'What were you thinking?'

'That I must be barking mad to be careering about in the dark on a cold winter's morning in my nightgown,' she said wryly.

'I only hope you don't come down with something.' He wrapped her in the blanket, puppy and all, and escorted her through the back door. 'Sophie's out to the world—snoring, would you believe?—so I'll just see you back safely to the cottage, then nip back to bed for an hour. I strongly advise you to do the same. Put the dog in her bed in the kitchen and shut yourself in your own room with the covers over your ears.'

Once she was back at the cottage and Miles had gone back to the house Elinor did as he said, managing to install the puppy in her own basket while she was still asleep. She crept up to her own room, shut the door and dived into bed, and went to sleep in seconds. Two hours later when Elinor went downstairs the puppy greeted her with joyous yelps, bouncing like a ball in her enthusiasm.

'Yes, I love you too. And I know you're cute and irresistible, but you're also a dog and you sleep downstairs,' said Elinor firmly, clipping the lead to Jet's collar. 'And no more dashing off like that, either, you hussy.'

After Elinor had cooked breakfast for the three of them Sophie assented eagerly when Miles said their first task was some shopping, then they would fetch Meg from the kennels.

'I hope she likes Jet,' said Sophie anxiously.

'You never know, Meg may teach her some manners,' said Miles, rescuing a floorcloth Jet had found in the larder. 'We'll buy her a leather bone to gnaw on, but first we help Elinor clear away and then you can take Jet out for a walk so she behaves while we're out.'

Elinor, who was getting used to mopping up puddles, nobly offered to stay at home with Jet while the other two went out.

'No, Nell,' said Sophie with gratifying vehemence. 'We want you to come too, don't we, Daddy?'

'We certainly do,' said Miles promptly, and smiled at Elinor. 'Carried unanimously.'

Elinor, who felt rather more appealing in a pink sweater and jeans than in the nightgown and rubber boots of their earlier encounter, smiled back, pleased. 'Then of course I'll come. Only Jet probably won't like the car ride.'

'I'll cuddle her,' said Sophie firmly. 'Then she won't mind. I'll take her walkies now.'

'On the croquet lawn, then,' said Miles. 'Keep away from the cliff path.'

'All right.' Sophie let Elinor button her into her duffel coat, coughing a little. 'Do I have to wear this?'

'It's pretty cold out there, darling. You can always take it off in the car if you want.'

'OK.' Sophie went off with the puppy, very careful to keep firm hold of the lead as instructed, and Miles watched her from the window.

'She likes you, Elinor.'

'I hope so.' She tugged on her sheepskin jacket. 'It's something one can't force. Children either like you or they don't.'

'Do you like Sophie?' he asked quietly.

She stared at him in astonishment. 'Of course I do. How could I help it? She looks——' She stopped dead.

'What were you going to say?'

Elinor had been about to say that Sophie looked so like her father it was impossible not to take to the little girl. 'She looks a little vulnerable sometimes,' she said instead, which was the perfect truth. 'When she gets a certain look in her eyes I want to hug her like mad until it goes.'

'I know exactly what you mean,' said Miles grimly. 'Fortunately the wariness is a lot less in evidence since she came here to live with me. It's just security, I suppose. I'm here all the time. She never knew when she'd see Selina.'

'But she must miss her mother.'

'Less than I expected. She's always a bit down after Selina talks to her on the phone, but I'm never quite sure whether that's due to what her mother says or to what she fails to say. Selina is not a demonstrative mother,' finished Miles without inflexion. 'So please hug Sophie as much as you like.'

Elinor smiled as the child came running back in with the puppy. 'Was she a good girl, Sophie?'

Sophie assured them that the puppy had done everything expected of her, and asked for a drink of water.

'I'm thirsty,' she said, after swallowing a beakerful. 'Look, Jet's thirsty too.' The puppy was gulping down so much water that Elinor felt sure another 'walkie' would be necessary before they even got in the car.

The shopping expedition was of necessity brief since Sophie elected to stay in the car with the puppy, and shortly afterwards they collected Meg from the kennels. For a while there was pandemonium in the Range Rover, but eventually Meg came to terms with the small, ingratiating creature.

'Jet's missing her mummy,' said Sophie, smiling wistfully. 'See? She's snuggling up to Meg.'

Back at Cliff house, Miles and Sophie took the dogs for a romp in the garden while Elinor put the groceries away and made a start on lunch. The menu, as eagerly requested, was burgers and beans with ice-cream to follow, but halfway through the meal Sophie pushed her plate away, leaving much of the food uneaten.

Elinor eyed it in dismay. It had taken no skill to prepare, but Sophie had so obviously disliked the meal that she felt strangely hurt.

'I'm not hungry,' said Sophie in distress, when Miles questioned her. 'I *like* burgers and beans best of all, but I feel sort of funny, Daddy.'

Elinor jumped up to touch the little girl's forehead. 'You're a bit hot, darling. In a minute perhaps you'd like a nice bath, then you can lie on the sofa in the study in your pyjamas and dressing-gown.'

Sophie nodded apathetically. 'OK. But what about Jet?'

'Don't worry,' said Miles, exchanging a worried look with Elinor over the shiny dark head. 'I'll see to her walk. And in any case she's much happier now Meg's back.'

Which was very true. The Irish wolfhound could hardly move for Jet, who lolloped after her everywhere. The older dog had beautiful manners and put up with it so good-naturedly that Sophie was eventually reconciled to leaving Jet behind when she went up for her bath.

'She'll be all right now,' Elinor assured her.

Sophie nodded, coughing drily. 'She likes Meg. Meg likes her too, doesn't she?'

'Of course she does, darling.' Elinor helped the child undress, eyeing the flushed cheeks and heavy eyes with foreboding as Sophie began to shiver. 'Perhaps we won't bother with the bath after all,' she said quickly, and pulled on Sophie's pyjamas at top speed before wrapping her in her scarlet wool dressing-gown. 'Right. Let's go down by the fire in the study.'

Tears welled in Sophie's eyes. 'I feel all hot and achy, Nell.'

'Oh, darling, do you?' Elinor cuddled her close. 'Would you prefer to pop into bed for a bit?'

To her dismay Sophie nodded, then gave a little sob. 'But I don't want to be on my own. Will you come too, Nell? Please?'

'You bet I will! Right, then, quick march.' She hurried her drooping little charge along the landing to her room, tucked her under the flowered quilt, then smoothed the hair back from Sophie's flushed face. 'I'm just going downstairs to get a hot-water bottle and tell Daddy where you are, then I'll be back. OK?'

'OK.'

Miles leapt up from the kitchen table as Elinor came into the room. 'What's wrong?'

She explained tersely as she filled the kettle and without a word Miles shot from the kitchen and took the stairs two at a time. When she reached Sophie's room he was sitting on his little daughter's bed, stroking her hair and trying to make her laugh by telling her that Jet had almost fallen in her bowl when she was gobbling her lunch. When a wan smile was his only reward he exchanged a worried look with Elinor as she tucked the hot-water bottle at Sophie's feet.

'Perhaps you could fetch up a tray with some drinks,' suggested Elinor calmly. 'Bottled water, orange juice, that kind of thing.'

'Lemonade?' said Sophie drowsily.

'Right,' said her father, pulling an armchair up to the bed. 'This is for you, Nell. Sophie says you're going to sit with her for a bit.'

'That's right. Thank you.' Elinor smiled cheerfully. 'I'll just go and wash my hands first.'

Outside in the upper hall Miles hurried her along until they were out of earshot. 'She's got a temperature.'

'I know. Pity my parents are away. Call the doctor anyway, Miles.'

'I was just about to.' He held her hands tightly.

She smiled reassuringly. 'Try not to worry. Children run temperatures very easily.'

He kissed the tip of her nose fleetingly. 'Right. I'll ring first, then bring those drinks up. Thank you, Nell.'

'What for?'

'Just for being here.'

Sophie was dozing when Elinor went back, her cheeks a hectic scarlet and dark marks under her closed eyes. Settling herself in the big old armchair, Elinor sat quietly, hoping the child wasn't suffering some kind of relapse after the chicken-pox.

It was odd how fate landed one in such unexpected situations, she reflected wearily, feeling the toll of several nights' broken sleep. Other than listening avidly to whatever snippets of news her mother passed on about him she hadn't given Miles Carew much thought once her hero-worshipping days were over. Now her life was suddenly so bound up with his it would be difficult to revert to normal once it wasn't. But if you're going to work for him you'll see him every day, a voice said in her head. Sophie too.

She looked up as Miles backed into the room with a loaded tray, and Sophie stirred.

'Thirsty,' she said hoarsely.

'Right you are, madam,' said Miles cheerfully, and poured out some fizzy lemonade. Elinor heaved the little girl up and stacked pillows behind her so that her father could give her the drink.

Sophie drained the glass thirstily, then sagged back against the pillows. 'Did you bring Nell a drink too, Daddy?'

'Of course,' he said, mock-offended. 'I brought her a whole pot of tea to herself.'

Elinor smiled gratefully. 'That was very thoughtful of you.'

'Books, too. I thought nurse might fancy a read.' His face shadowed as Sophie relapsed into sleep once more.

'I know they sleep a lot when they're off colour,' he said in an undertone. 'I found that out when she had chicken-pox. If it's any consolation to you, Nell, I could ring Sandy Reid's blasted neck right now. If it hadn't been for him she could have convalesced in peace instead of being shunted off to Ludlow.'

Elinor nodded. 'Did you ring the practice?'

'Yes. One of the doctors will call before evening surgery.' He stared down at his daughter. 'She looks hellish fragile, Elinor.'

'If she's anything like her father—and I'm sure she is—she's a tough little cookie.' She smiled at him comfortingly. 'I'll stay with her, Miles. And I'll call if she wants you. I hate to remind you but Jet probably needs an airing.'

He gave a wry grin as he turned reluctantly from his child. 'Right. I'll take the dogs out and try to get Meg to demonstrate exactly where and how puddles should be made—as far from the house as possible!' He brushed a hand over Elinor's hair then left her to pour herself a cup of tea. She chose a thriller from the books he'd brought her, looked across anxiously at Sophie, then settled down to her vigil.

CHAPTER EIGHT

SOPHIE, the doctor confirmed, had influenza coupled with a touch of bronchitis. He prescribed antibiotics and some soothing linctus, said the usual things about plenty of fluids and not to expect any appetite until the temperature was down. He expressed no surprise at finding Elinor installed at Cliff House, commented that some of her parents' medical knowledge was bound to have rubbed off over the years, and told Miles not to worry. Sophie had probably contracted flu due to her weakened resistance after the recent dose of chicken-pox.

'She must have caught it in Ludlow, like Tom,' said Miles grimly once the brisk young man had gone. 'If she'd been allowed to stay at home she'd probably be fine.'

Elinor, who agreed whole-heartedly, didn't contradict him. If she'd had Alexander Reid in reach at that moment she'd have made him cry all right, she thought fiercely as she sponged Sophie's hot forehead.

It was the beginning of a week of misery for the child and mounting exhaustion for Elinor. Miles's whipcord strength was more than equal to the physical tasks, but he was so worried that Elinor expended a lot of her own energy in reassuring him that his child would soon be well.

She took charge of the laundry since Sophie's fever meant bouts of sickness and drenching sweats which needed frequent changes of bed-linen. Her meagre wardrobe was soon sorely tried. Leaving Miles in charge, she went down to the cottage one morning and ransacked both her own and her mother's belongings for supplies of clean underwear, shirts, sweaters, anything to ease the situation.

Sleep became a thing of the past. Even when Miles sat up with Sophie Elinor couldn't rest, and eventually after three days, she gave up trying.

'Look, there's no point in both of us going without sleep,' she said firmly. 'I'd rather doze here in the chair with Sophie. I just can't settle in bed.'

'But you'll be worn out, Nell,' argued Miles. 'Can't you just get in my bed for a while and crash out? I promise I'll come for you if she wants you.'

Which was the crux of the problem. Sophie wanted Elinor all the time. She drifted in and out of sleep, but now and again would start awake and look wildly for Elinor, then breathe out a sigh of relief when she found her there at the bedside, ready with a drink or just a cool, reassuring hand to take hold of the small, damp hot one lying limply on the quilt.

Sophie was happiest of all when Miles was there too. But her anxiety over the puppy was so great that she would sometimes start to cry, only calming down if he left at once, promising to make sure Jet was all right.

'I'd rather stay here,' said Elinor. 'Please, Miles.'

'I'm deeply grateful, Elinor. I don't know what we'd have done without you.' He smiled crookedly. 'Selina was never much use as a nurse.'

She must have been good at something, thought Elinor acidly.

By the end of the week Sophie had begun to mend. On Friday, Miles felt sufficiently reassured to go out for more groceries, leaving Sophie to her afternoon nap. Elinor stayed reading in the chair beside her, promising herself that when Miles got back she'd soak for a while in a hot bath, wash her hair, and generally make herself look more human again. Waking with a start from a doze, she heard the dogs barking and repeated peals on the front doorbell.

Sophie stirred, and Elinor laid a gentling hand on her forehead. 'Shan't be long, darling. Someone's at the door.'

Thrusting her hair back from her pallid face, she went wearily downstairs and along the hall. Through the glass panes of the upper half of the door she saw that the visitor waiting in the porch was a woman.

She unlocked the door and opened it, her heart sinking like a stone. The beautiful face and gleaming chestnut hair were unmistakable. Selina Carew had taken it into her head to make an unheralded visit to her daughter.

As Elinor held the door open the visitor brushed past into the hall, tall and striking in a white cashmere coat. 'Where's Major Carew, please?'

'I'm afraid he's out,' said Elinor, deeply conscious of her creased shirt and tatty sweater and leggings, which were all of a piece with her unwashed hair and haggard face.

'Are you Mrs Hedley's help?' demanded Selina, obviously finding it unnecessary to introduce herself to so lowly a mortal.

'No. I'm Elinor Gibson from next door.'

'Good heavens—the tomboy always in scrapes with Harry and Mark?' Selina eyed her up and down, making it obvious that Elinor hadn't improved her appearance in the interim.

'The very same,' said Elinor, her hackles rising under the amused blue scrutiny. 'Your daughter hasn't been well; I've been helping out.'

Selina frowned. 'Sophie not well? What do you mean?'

'She's got flu.'

'Is it infectious?'

'Probably not, by now.'

'What do you mean, "by now"?' demanded Selina. 'How long has she been ill?'

Elinor explained, and Selina scowled. 'Really! You'd think Miles would have taken more care of her. Where's Mrs Hedley?'

When she learned the Hedleys weren't in residence Selina's beautiful mouth tightened. 'Where is Sophie? Take me to her at once.'

'She's in her usual bedroom,' said Elinor quietly.

Selina's chin lifted. 'I'm afraid I don't know which one it is. I haven't been here since Sophie was born.'

Elinor turned towards the stairs. 'This way, please.'

'Lord, I'd forgotten what a barracks of a place this is,' said Selina as she followed Elinor along the upper hall, past ranks of bedroom doors. 'What it must cost to heat it I can't imagine.'

'Selina's in here,' said Elinor, opening the last door.

Selina swept into the room on a cloud of perfume, her famous smile fading as she saw the small, fragile figure lying in the bed. 'Sophie! Angel! What on earth have they done to you?'

Sophie stared at her mother in astonishment, tears of weakness welling up in her dark-ringed eyes. 'Mummy?' she said questioningly, as though her mother were a figment of the imagination.

'Of course it's Mummy, darling.' Selina sat down gingerly on the edge of the bed. 'I hear you've got flu, poppet. What terribly bad luck.'

Elinor, who'd been expecting Selina to sweep her little daughter into her arms, stood quietly by the door, her heart contracting as she watched Sophie mop her own tears from the box of tissues lying on the bed beside her.

Suddenly the door opened and Miles came into the room, then stopped short, his face blank with amazement.

'*Selina*?'

'Miles!' In one fluid movement Selina rose to her feet and melted gracefully into the arms he closed involuntarily around her. She smiled up into his surprised face and pressed a lingering kiss on his mouth, and Elinor watched with sudden, searing pain. 'I acted on impulse and appeared without warning, I'm afraid,' said Selina, caressing his cheek with stroking, red-tipped fingers. 'A good thing I did, too,' she added, turning back to Sophie, 'by the look of my poor little darling here.'

Elinor tried to slide unseen from the room, but Miles released Selina to stay her with a forceful hand. 'As it happens Sophie's had the best care possible. Elinor here hasn't been to bed for nights—spent the whole time in this room with Sophie.'

'So I see,' said Selina, looking Elinor up and down in distaste. 'Why on earth didn't you hire a professional nurse, Miles? I hear you've funds enough these days.'

Suddenly Sophie started to cry in earnest. Elinor started towards her, but Selina pushed her aside. 'If you don't mind,' she said sweetly, and, at last, took her child in her arms. 'There, there, darling, don't cry. Mummy's here now.'

Cut to pieces, one way and another, Elinor ignored Miles's outstretched hand and went blindly from the room. Once outside in the corridor she ran along the hall and down the stairs to the kitchen to snatch up her coat. After a moment's hesitation, she shook her head at the importuning puppy.

'You stay here with Meg,' she said huskily. 'Sophie will worry if I take you away.'

Once inside Cliff Cottage Elinor ran a bath and lay in it up to her ears, too tired to cry. She heard the telephone ring but couldn't bring herself to get out to answer it. Sophie, after all, was safe in the elegant arms of her mother, a lady to whom Miles, it seemed, wasn't nearly as indifferent as he made out. Falling in love, she reminded herself, was something Miles had done with Selina. He'd told her so himself. And never said a word about falling back out of it again.

Eventually, drained of all emotion other than relief at feeling clean, she sat drying her hair until it shone again in all its usual variations of colour. She tied it back with a ribbon, pulled on an old yellow sweater of her mother's, and found that after the stress of the past few days she could squeeze into a pair of jeans from her teenage era. While she was buckling her belt she saw lights sweep past and ran to the window to see a familiar car driving up the back way to Cliff House. Thank heaven—the Hedleys were back.

She relaxed a little. She could leave them all to it now with a clear conscience. Unless, said a hateful small voice, Sophie wakes up in the night and cries for you. With her mother there? she retorted with sarcasm. In your dreams, Elinor Gibson!

Most of her clothes, and quite a few of her mother's, she remembered, biting her lip, were still in various stages of laundering up at Cliff House. She sighed. They'd just have to stay there while Selina Carew was in residence. And now the Hedleys were back Jet would be no problem to Miles either. Tom would exercise her with Meg. Elinor Gibson's presence, one way and another, was totally superfluous.

To her surprise she found she was hungry. She'd eaten very little during the past few days, too worried about Sophie to have much appetite—and too tired. Still too tired to bother much, she made some tea, toasted the stale remains of the loaf and topped it with some melted cheese, then took a tray into the sitting-room to eat her meal in front of the television news. The weather, she was informed at the end of it, was improving rapidly, with rising temperatures and clear, sunny skies promised nationwide for the next few days. Which meant clear roads and railways and nothing to prevent her return to Cheltenham.

When the phone rang later Elinor got up reluctantly to answer it, unsurprised to hear Miles's voice.

'Elinor, are you all right? Why did you dash off like that?'

'I needed a bath. How's Sophie?'

'Still recovering from the shock of seeing her mother, I think. But she's asking for you. Will you come up this evening and see her? The Hedleys are back and Mrs H is cooking the fatted calf. I want you to come and share it with us.'

The mere thought of sitting at table with Selina Carew gave Elinor violent indigestion. 'No, thanks, Miles. I've just had some supper. Once I was clean I discovered I was a bit hungry. And I saw the Hedleys arrive so I knew you—and Sophie—were in good hands.'

'Just because the Hedleys are back it doesn't mean Sophie and I don't need you here, Elinor,' he said impatiently.

'Under the circumstances I think it's best if I leave you to it for a while. Tell Sophie I'll come and see her when—when——'

'When her mother's gone,' said Miles grimly.

'Well, yes.' Elinor swallowed. 'Does your—does Selina intend staying for a while?'

'I don't know.' Miles paused. 'Under the circumstances I can't refuse her time with Sophie.'

'Of course not. Would you mind hanging on to Jet for a while, please? I thought I'd go back to Cheltenham to sort things out there.'

'I'll do anything you ask, always, Elinor,' he assured her, in a tone which brought a lump to her throat.

'Thank you,' she said with difficulty. 'Ask Sophie to take care of her for me once she's well.'

'I'll take care of her, don't worry. Selina wants to take Sophie away for a couple of weeks before rehearsals start for the new serial. I'd rather she didn't, but I could hardly refuse.'

'I suppose not. How does Sophie feel about it?'

'I haven't broached the subject yet. Elinor, listen——'

'Sorry, I must go. Someone's ringing my doorbell. Goodbye, Miles, love to Sophie.' Elinor put down the phone, scrubbing furiously at her wet eyes, then went to open the door.

The man with his hand raised halfway to the bell looked at her in appalled surprise as he saw her face under the light. 'Elinor! What in heaven's name have you done to yourself?'

'Oliver!' she said faintly.

A few minutes later Elinor took a tray of coffee into the sitting-room and gave Oliver permission to light one of his cigars.

'I know your parents disapprove,' he said wryly, 'but in their absence and in the circumstances I feel I should be allowed one, darling, don't you?'

Elinor nodded. 'Of course.'

'So I can't change your mind, Elinor,' he said, regarding her through a blue haze of smoke.

Elinor smiled at him. Oliver looked elegant, as always, in a magnificent dark suit and a spotted burgundy silk tie knotted at the collar of his cream silk shirt. 'No, I'm afraid not. But I hope we can still be friends.'

He grimaced. 'You might have spared me that old chestnut, darling.'

'I mean it just the same,' she assured him, and he smiled ruefully.

'I know you do. To be honest I'd been expecting my marching orders for some time—which didn't make it easier to take, alas, when it happened. Sorry I was less than gracious. I'm too old and set in my ways for you, I suppose, Elinor. Your chums make me feel like Methuselah. And I thoroughly enjoy socialising with intent, as you put it, to make contacts for the firm. My mistake was in expecting you to enjoy it too. End of speech, darling. Now tell me what I can do for you.'

'Could you take me back to Cheltenham tonight?'

Oliver fixed her with shrewd eyes. 'You mean you've tired of rural isolation?'

'Something like that.'

'Then I shall be delighted, of course.' He frowned at her. 'You really do look terrible, you know. And yes, I know you've been nursing a friend's child and so on, but I fancy there's rather more to it than that.'

Knowing the probing qualities of Oliver's legal mind, Elinor decided to take him into her confidence and tell him the dramatic, improbable story of the siege at Cliff House.

He was startled out of his normal aplomb early on in her account. 'Is this for real, Elinor? You mean Carew let the devil off in the end?'

She nodded. 'Fellow officers and all that. Miles could understand the workings of the man's mind— felt sorry for him when Captain Reid broke down and sobbed on his shoulder.'

'Carew should have prosecuted,' said Oliver heatedly. 'My God, Elinor, you could have been killed. No wonder you look like death.'

'I'll soon be my usual glowing self,' she told him cheerfully. 'Incidentally, if you'd like me to come back and work for you, I will—unless you'd find that embarrassing now.'

'Not on your life, darling! I'm delighted.' He eyed her keenly. 'But I thought you had another job lined up.'

Her eyes fell. 'I've changed my mind.'

'Does that mean,' he said thoughtfully, 'you might—in time—change your mind about marrying me too?'

Elinor gave him an affectionate smile. 'No, Oliver, it doesn't. I don't think I'm cut out for marriage, somehow.'

'I can't say I agree with that,' he said lightly, and glanced at his watch. 'If you're coming with me I imagine you'll have things to do, so I'll watch some mindless diversion on your television while you pack.'

She took very little time to get ready, since most of her belongings were still up at Cliff House. She rang Linda to tell her of the new arrangement, then, on the point of ringing Miles, changed her mind. Her heart contracted as a vision of Sophie's vulnerable little face suddenly flashed into her mind, vivid with reproach. '*Et tu, Brute*?' she asked herself bitterly.

With a sigh she got up and went downstairs. 'Oliver, I'd better not come back tonight after all. If you'll take my things I'll follow on tomorrow by train.'

'Of course.' He picked up her overnight bag. 'Am I allowed to ask why the change of plan?'

'I need to say goodbye to a very sick little girl in the morning. I was going to leave a message, but I just can't take off without seeing her. Six-year-olds get hurt very easily.'

'Not only six-year-olds,' he said pensively, and smiled to belie the words. 'Just joking, Elinor. So the sick child in question belongs to Major Carew?'

She nodded. 'I've been nursing her through a bad dose of flu. Her mother's arrived on the scene now, so I'm not needed any more, but I just can't steal off without saying goodbye to Sophie.'

*   *   *

When Oliver had gone Elinor sat down and made herself face facts. In her teens she'd been in love with the idea of Miles Carew—something fostered by the smart uniform, the aura of glamour about his activities in the army. But he'd married young and eventually she'd relinquished the dream. Then fate had thrown them together again, and now she felt a strong resentment against it for doing something so cruel— because it wasn't all she felt, by a long shot. She was harrowed by pity for Sophie, jealous of Selina, and deeply, irrevocably in love with Miles Carew.

All in all, she told herself scathingly, she was a fool. She should have gone off with Oliver tonight, she knew very well. And it wasn't just the thought of Sophie's wan little face which had kept her back, if she was totally honest. She just couldn't bear to go away without one last meeting with Miles. Miles, the man who at this very minute was probably having a fun evening with his glamorous ex-wife.

Elinor jumped to her feet restlessly and went out to the kitchen to make coffee, unable to bear the thought of Selina with Miles. She filled a kettle, then leaned moodily against the counter as she waited for it to boil, so deep in abstraction that she jumped out of her skin at a sudden knock on the kitchen door. Her heart banged in her chest as she recognised the familiar tattoo.

'Elinor?' called Miles from outside. 'Open up. It's me.'

For a childish moment Elinor was tempted to let him stay outside, pretend she hadn't heard, then common sense, along with a few other emotions, sent her to the door. She slid back the bolts and opened it. Miles, in the familiar parka, stood outside, holding Jet and Meg on leashes.

She looked at him for a long moment.

'Can we come in?' he asked, as the puppy bounced up and down like a rubber ball in greeting.

Without a word Elinor held the door wide, and Miles handed over the leashes to her and bent to remove his boots. She crouched down with the dogs, making a great fuss of both of them to hide her agitation. Something about him made it plain that Miles intended staying longer than just a minute or two. He straightened, divested himself of the parka, hung it on a peg, then unclipped the dogs' leads.

'I'd like a word, please, Elinor,' he said shortly, and closed the kitchen door on the dogs, commanding them to stay.

'You'd better come into the sitting-room,' she said with composure, and led the way. She curled up in a corner of the sofa, gesturing to one of the chintz-covered chairs graciously. 'Do sit down.'

Miles, however, preferred to stand, towering over her in the low-ceilinged room. 'When I was out with the dogs earlier I saw a car in the drive.'

Her chin lifted. 'Yes, you did.'

'Who was it?'

She stared up at him coldly. 'Why do you have to know that? Are you the only one allowed visitors?'

His eyes gleamed. 'I didn't ask Selina to come.'

'I didn't ask Oliver to come, either.'

'I was right, then. I assumed a Mercedes must be the ex-fiancé's style.' Miles's eyes narrowed suddenly. 'Or is he no longer ex?'

'I might ask the same about Selina!' The moment the words were out of her mouth Elinor regretted them, and hastily, before he could answer, she asked after Sophie.

'She took a long time to settle down. Very tearful and crotchety, I'm afraid. It took the combined efforts of Mrs Hedley and myself to get her to sleep.' He eyed her accusingly. 'She couldn't understand why you were missing.'

Elinor paled, speared by a sharp pang of remorse. 'I thought once she had her mother she wouldn't need me.'

His eyes bored down into hers. 'Did you, Elinor? Truthfully? Or did you go off in a very understandable huff because my ex-wife was so rude to you?'

'Please sit down, Miles,' she said irritably. 'I can't talk with you looming over me like that.'

He sat down on the edge of the sofa, half turned towards her.

'Didn't Selina help with settling Sophie down for the night?' she couldn't help asking.

'No. She got annoyed when Sophie kept asking for you.' Miles shrugged. 'Sophie got in such a state I came down for you at that point, but then I saw the car and realised I was out of luck.'

'I would have come if I'd known Sophie needed me.'

He shrugged again. 'It seemed too much of an imposition. So I went back and told her you had visitors and you'd come and see her in the morning. I'm here now to confirm the arrangement.' His eyes met hers. 'I wondered if I'd find you here, and, if I did, whether you'd be alone.'

CHAPTER NINE

The silence in the room was almost tangible. After a moment Elinor couldn't bear it.

'I fully intended going back tonight with Oliver. To Cheltenham, I mean, to my own flat,' she added in a rush. 'But I couldn't leave without saying goodbye to Sophie. I'll come and see her in the morning.'

'And afterwards I take it you *are* going back,' he said expressionlessly. 'To Oliver?'

'Yes.'

His face set intimidatingly. 'I see.'

'To work for him again, nothing more.'

'I thought you were going to work for me!'

'After today I realise that just isn't practical.'

His brows flew together. 'Why the hell not?'

She raised her chin. 'Due to an extraordinary set of circumstances you and I got suddenly involved, Miles. And then Sophie got ill and we got more involved than ever in a different kind of way. But you're obviously still in love with, or at the very least still lust after, Selina. And I can't handle that.

'I don't blame you. She's even more beautiful in the flesh than on screen. But before I get any more involved I'm backing out. Which doesn't mean I'm abandoning Sophie. I promise I'll come back and visit her regularly when my parents are home. I'll do my best to make her understand——'

'Good! Because then perhaps she'll be able to explain to me,' he said viciously, and seized Elinor's hands. 'Because I bloody well do *not* understand. And as for lusting after Selina, you couldn't be more wrong.'

'Rubbish—I saw you with her today,' retorted Elinor hotly. 'You weren't exactly fighting her off when she kissed you. *Miles*—you're hurting me.'

He flung her hands away.

'All right,' he said after a while. 'What, exactly, did you imagine you saw?'

'I saw how you—how you reacted when she kissed you,' she said, her eyes falling. 'You told me once that Selina was the only one you'd ever fallen in love with. I think you're *still* in love with her.'

He maintained an oddly menacing silence, looking at her in a way which made her deeply uneasy. She fidgeted for a while, then gradually stilled, hypnotised by the mounting intensity in his narrowed eyes.

'What, I wonder,' he said softly at last, 'can I do to convince you how wrong you are?'

Suddenly he moved like lightning, and caught Elinor fast in a pair of arms which held her like steel bands. She fought against them in immediate reflex action, but his arms tightened like a vice and she gasped, and Miles stopped her open mouth with his, stifling her protests with a controlled savagery which both scared her stiff and set her senses alight.

He stood up with her in his arms and, impervious to her struggles, strode from the room and mounted the stairs with an ease which made it frighteningly obvious that carrying a hundred and twenty pounds of girl was child's play to someone able to walk sixty miles with over two hundred pounds of equipment on his back.

When he reached her room he kicked the door open and dumped her on the bed, breathing hard—but with something very different from effort, Elinor saw with panic. She scrambled away from him but he caught her and flipped her on her back, imprisoning both her hands above her head with one of his.

'You were right about the lusting,' he said very softly. 'But wrong about who I was lusting for. I meant this to happen later on in our relationship, but it can't wait any longer. Neither,' he added, his breath searing her lips, 'can I.'

'Stop it,' she gasped, trying in vain to twist away. '*Please*! You'll be sorry——'

'*You* may be,' he interrupted through his teeth, and let go her hands, but only to strip her sweater over her head. 'I won't.'

Elinor began to fight in earnest, but Miles was much taller, also a lot heavier—despite his slim, wiry build—and trained to subdue far more difficult opposition than a girl whose only exercise was done to music. The unequal battle was soon over, and the moment they were both naked he took immediate possession of her body. To her shame he accomplished this with humiliating ease.

It was the last straw. Tears of rage and humiliation poured down her face as Miles made love to her with a combination of ferocity and skill which brought her to a culmination of such convulsive, overwhelming pleasure that his eyes blazed with triumph into hers in the seconds before he met the same fate. Then at last it was over and her body was her own again, instead of some instrument Miles Carew had played on to such devastating effect.

Elinor lay flat on her back with an arm thrown over her closed eyes, feeling as though her entire body was one great hammering pulse. She willed him to go away but instead he lay on his stomach beside her, one long leg thrown over hers in casual possession. It was a long time before her breathing slowed. Afterwards the silence lengthened until she could stand it no longer.

'Go away now, please,' she said at last, her voice flat with suppressed emotion.

'No.'

Elinor took her arm away, opening her eyes directly into the gleam in his as Miles raised his head to look at her. In the faint light from the landing the look of triumphant satisfaction on his face was all too easy to see.

'Are you convinced?' he demanded.

'Of what?' she said scornfully. 'That you're bigger and stronger than me? That you can subdue me with a weapon I don't possess? Big deal!'

'Is that all I did? Subdue?'

Elinor contemplated lying, and decided against it. 'No, you know very well it wasn't,' she said wearily.

'Do you want me to apologise?'

Her eyes flashed. 'What good would that do? The damage is done.'

He smoothed her tangled hair, and she shied away from his touch angrily. 'The only real damage, Nell, was to your pride.'

'My *pride*?'

He nodded. 'I set out to convince you exactly who it was I wanted, and how much. But it wasn't rape. At the end you couldn't hide what happened to you.'

Probably, she thought bitterly, because it had never happened before. She'd always faked it with Oliver. Apparently it was harder to fake the other way round.

'You'd better get back to Sophie,' she said, trying to move. The leg impeded her, joined by an arm which rendered her even more immobile.

'Mrs Hedley's staying with Sophie until I get back.'

'Why not Selina?'

'Selina's departed for the time being, Elinor.'

'Departed?'

'Lloyd Forbes took her back to Chepstow after a rather eventful dinner.'

'Selina's new man?' Elinor blinked, trying to clear her head. 'When did *he* arrive on the scene?'

'He drove Selina here in the first place. Dropped her off at the house, then went to register at the George and came back to join us for a meal to celebrate their recent wedding in Antigua.'

'Oh.' Elinor's smile was scornful. 'The three of you together. How very civilised.'

'It was a total bloody disaster. I had to go upstairs every few minutes to Sophie. Lloyd got more and more impatient, and in the end Selina went off with him.' He tightened his hold as he felt Elinor stir. 'They're staying on in Chepstow for a day or two to make arrangements for Sophie's holiday.'

'And how does Sophie feel about that?'

'At the moment, poor baby, she's confused. She adored the *idea* of Mummy turning up like the good fairy. But how long Selina can sustain the role is open to question. For Sophie's sake I hope it outlasts the holiday.' He stroked her cheek with a caressing finger. 'The ideal arrangement, from Sophie's point of view, would be for you to go on holiday with them too.'

Elinor shuddered at the mere idea of it. Not even for Sophie could she make that sacrifice. She pushed at Miles. 'Will you please go away now? I'm cold and I want to get some clothes on.'

For answer Miles drew up the quilt and covered them both, holding her tightly. 'Not just yet. Sophie's sleeping, and Tom will ring if Mrs Hedley needs me. I want you just where you are, right here in my arms for a while.'

Elinor shoved him away. 'Frankly, Miles Carew, you've got a nerve, after...'

'After what?' said Miles, recapturing her with ease. 'After making love to you?'

She lay still in his arms. 'Because you did it as some kind of demonstration,' she said bitterly. 'You made love to me as a punishment, not because you really wanted to.'

'Of course I wanted to,' he said scathingly. 'Almost from the first moment we met up again, if you want times and dates.' He pulled her to him and kissed her at length. 'And now,' he said against her mouth, '*not* by way of demonstration, but because, as is all too obvious, I want you again right now. And this time I'm going to make love to you very, very slowly, until you beg for mercy.'

Elinor made a token lunge for freedom for pride's sake, not really wanting to escape, but Miles held her fast as he began to kiss her again, his strategy for this second assault infinitely more subtle than the first. Quieting her token resistance with stroking, gentling hands, he kissed her with a hungry, mounting tenderness which left her defenceless. And afterwards the shared days of strain suddenly caught up with them, and with no further exchange, spoken or otherwise, they fell deeply asleep in each other's arms.

Elinor stirred eventually to the sounds of barking and voices; she swam up from the depths of sleep, blinking owlishly as the overhead light went on, and then stared, transfixed, her eyes wide with horrified embarrassment, as she saw the astounded faces of her parents.

'Mother? Dad?' she faltered, and extricated herself from the arms of the man beside her. Miles sat up, looking somewhat dishevelled but otherwise totally at ease.

'*Miles*?' said Mary Gibson blankly. 'I—I assumed it was Oliver...'

'Elinor's not engaged to Maynard any more,' said Miles Carew helpfully, and turned to smile at the scarlet, embarrassed girl in the bed beside him as she yanked the covers up under her chin.

'Damned good thing under the circumstances,' said Dr Henry Gibson with gruff emphasis, and took his wife's arm. 'Come downstairs, Mary; let these two get dressed.'

'What date is it?' asked Elinor frantically as the door closed on her parents.

Miles took a look at his watch. 'March 4th.'

'They weren't due back until next week,' she wailed, suddenly galvanised into action. 'For heaven's sake get your clothes on and get out of here. Oh, glory, the dogs! I bet Jet's made puddles all over the kitchen floor.'

'Calm down,' said Miles, dressing at top speed. 'I'll make the necessary explanations and apologies——'

'No, you won't,' she said fiercely, desperately trying to locate garments Miles had thrown far and wide earlier. She dragged a brush through her hair, eyeing her flushed face in despair. 'I'm a grown woman. It isn't a hanging matter because I had a man in my room. I just wish it hadn't been you!'

'Why? Would they prefer it was Maynard?'

'Of course they would! I was supposed to be marrying him, remember,' she snapped, and took a deep breath. 'Oh, dear. Let's get this over with.'

Miles thrust her aside. 'I'll go first. I got you into this.' And, deaf to her protests, he ran downstairs and went into the kitchen where Mrs Gibson, just as Elinor predicted, was busily mopping up a puddle.

'Henry's taken the dogs for a very necessary walk—I assume the puppy's yours, Miles,' she said serenely. 'I've put the kettle on. Anyone for coffee?'

With sublime disregard for the situation she'd interrupted in her daughter's bedroom Mary Gibson explained the early return from Australia. Her sister had bought some very expensive raffle tickets at a charity concert, and won the first prize of a holiday for two in Hawaii.

'This week and next were the times specified, so we packed Rose and Jeff off—after a certain amount of protest—then rearranged our flight, had a couple of days on our own in Sydney, and flew home. The plane was delayed or we'd have been home earlier.'

Dr Gibson came back into the kitchen with the dogs, shivering. 'Damned chilly here after the weather out there.' He fixed Miles with a cold, hostile stare. 'Sold you my house, Major; I didn't throw in my daughter.'

'*Dad!*' said Elinor, incensed.

'Your father's entitled to an explanation,' said Miles reasonably.

'Not really.' Henry Gibson shook his head, thawing somewhat. 'I might have been a few generations back. But Elinor's a grown woman in charge of her own life. I won't say it doesn't go against the grain, but there's no point in coming the heavy father. Who she invites into her bed isn't our responsibility.'

'That's rather the point, sir,' said Miles, standing very erect. 'She didn't invite me. I forced the issue.'

'Is this true, Elinor?' demanded her mother, astonished.

'Well, yes, in a way...'

'Then I damn well do require an explanation,' said Dr Gibson grimly.

To Elinor's deep relief the telephone provided a welcome interruption, and after a quick word her mother handed the receiver over to Miles.

'Tom Hedley for you.'

Miles listened intently for a moment. 'Yes, Tom. Right. Tell her I'm on my way.'

'Sophie?' said Elinor anxiously.

'Yes. She's crying for me.' He shrugged on his parka.

'Does she want me too?'

'I'll explain that your parents are back—tell her you'll see her in the morning.' He looked from Dr Gibson to his wife. 'I'll defer my own explanations until tomorrow. But I'd like you to know I intend to marry Elinor, and hope I can count on your support to bring her round to the idea.'

The ensuing exclamations of surprise silenced any protests from Elinor until she was outside with Miles for a word in private. 'Why in the wide world did you say that?' she demanded furiously. 'It was complicated enough before.'

'It's the simple truth,' said Miles, taking her breath away. 'I would have preferred more time to get you used to the idea, but having your parents surprise us *in flagrante* as it were, rather precipitated things.'

'You didn't have to say you'd marry me just because of that!' she said scornfully. 'You're in the wrong century.'

'We'll talk about it later,' said Miles. 'I must go.' Holding the dogs' leads with one hand, he pulled her to him with the other and kissed her long and hard, then let her go. 'Come up in the morning.'

CHAPTER TEN

ELINOR felt distinctly shaken as she went back into the house, and for the first time in her life was embarrassed at the thought of explanations to her parents.

'I've made some tea,' said Mrs Gibson, taking in the two flaring triangles of colour along Elinor's cheekbones. 'Your father's taken the luggage upstairs, so while we have a moment to ourselves tell me the truth. *Are* you going to marry Miles?'

'Certainly not,' said Elinor flatly. 'He had absolutely no right to say that.'

'To the casual onlooker in your room just now it seemed as though he had *some* right.' Mary Gibson smiled as she took Elinor in her arms and hugged her close. 'But never mind that for now—I've been so *worried* darling. We've tried to get hold of you for days. I rang the flat and eventually a strange man answered—Linda's boyfriend apparently. He just said you were away, so I eventually got in touch with Oliver and found you were here, but you never answered the phone. I rang earlier from the airport but still no luck, so in the end we collected the car and just turned up. It was quite a shock to find you with Miles.'

'I was surprised about it myself!' said Elinor with feeling, and looked up with an apologetic smile as her father came in, holding a glass of whisky. 'Sorry to embarrass you like that, Dad.'

Her father's eyes twinkled. 'Now I've had time to pull myself together I can see the funny side of it, darling.'

'Come on,' said his wife firmly. 'Let's go in the other room and make ourselves comfortable. Age and jet-lag are a lethal combination—I need lots of tea and my own special chair.'

Once they were settled Elinor took a deep breath and plunged into her story. 'I came running back here because I finished with Oliver. He didn't take too kindly to the idea——'

'Why did you finish it?' interrupted her mother gently.

Elinor sighed. 'I realised we just aren't right for each other.'

'He's a damn sight too old for you, for one thing,' said her father bluntly.

Elinor stared at him in surprise. 'You never said so before.'

'I wouldn't let him,' said Mrs Gibson. 'I was certain you'd find that out for yourself eventually.'

Elinor shook her head in wonder. 'This is a night for surprises! Anyway, I rushed home here to lick my wounds for a while—blissfully ignorant that you'd sold the house to Miles Carew, by the way,' she added accusingly.

Her father looked a little discomfited. 'He asked me to say nothing until it was all signed and sealed, and in the rush to get off on holiday I simply forgot to tell you.'

Elinor shrugged. 'Not that it matters now. But I've got quite a story to tell, one way and another.' She went on to explain the dramatic circumstances of her meeting with Miles in the snow, followed by a carefully edited version of the siege Alexander Reid had subjected them to.

'Good God!' said her father. 'Why the devil didn't Miles hand the maniac over to the police?'

Elinor explained the ex-army captain's nervous breakdown, and Miles's reluctance to aggravate it or to prosecute a fellow officer.

Mrs Gibson shuddered. 'I'm very glad I knew nothing about it.' She looked at her daughter curiously. 'So how did you cope on your own with Miles?'

'Very well.' Elinor gave her mother a rueful look. 'Too well, I suppose. The siege rather hurried our relationship on a bit. Then we got Sophie back and she's been so ill, poor darling, and—and——'

'You had another crisis to bind you even closer. Yet you don't seem very happy about Miles and this marriage idea.'

'I'm not.'

'Why? Do you mean you don't care for Miles enough to marry him?'

'Wrong way round, Mother. I don't think he cares enough for me.'

Dr Gibson frowned. 'Then why does he want to marry you?'

'His main reason is security for Sophie. And because Sophie likes having me around he's decided to marry me to acquire it for her.'

Mrs Gibson frowned. 'In that case, Elinor, think long and hard before you say yes.'

'Don't worry, I will.'

'When you said the wrong way round, darling, did you mean that you *do* love Miles?'

'Oh, yes. It isn't as if it's anything new, is it?' she said lightly. 'I always had a terrible crush on him. Meeting him again has just...well, revived it, I suppose.'

'I like Miles,' said Mrs Gibson. 'I think he's better suited to you than Oliver—more alive, somehow.'

Elinor scowled. 'If you mean Miles is more impetuous, I agree. There was absolutely no need for him to mention marriage. I told him he was living in the past.'

'I doubt that he feels obliged to,' said her father drily. 'He wasn't the least put out when we barged in on you like that. He was as cool as a cucumber—the only one who was.'

'Trained to keep his head in difficult situations.'

'I bet they didn't teach him that at Sandhurst!' He laughed, then gave her an apologetic look. 'Sorry I never got round to telling you Miles had bought the cottage.'

'It was a bit of a shock when he told me,' his daughter confessed. 'But I'm glad Sophie will be living here.'

'If you marry Miles you'll be living here too,' her mother pointed out.

'Well, I'm not, so I won't be.' Elinor got up. 'I'm going to bed. Tomorrow's likely to be a full day. I'm sorry to rush off the moment you're back, but in the circumstances I think I'd better get back to Cheltenham.'

'You mean you're running away?'

'You bet I am. It's the ideal moment to do it, too. Sophie's off with her mother on holiday, so she won't feel I'm deserting her.'

* * *

Her brief sleep in Miles's arms was all the rest Elinor was to get that night. She lay awake, between sheets which still seemed warm from his lovemaking, haunted by the certainty that he needed her more as a surrogate mother for his daughter than as a wife. That he wanted a physical relationship with her as part of the package she no longer had any doubt. But marriage with a man who was fond of her, instead of loving her as she wanted so badly to be loved by Miles Carew, sounded like a recipe for heartbreak. It was better to make the break now, while she could, at a time when Sophie would suffer the least harm from it.

You could always marry him first and try to make him love you later, suggested a voice in her mind. And if I didn't succeed I'd be heartbroken, she replied to it firmly. Besides, love was something which happened naturally or didn't, as the case might be. As she knew to her cost. She'd tried to love Oliver but it hadn't worked—whereas she'd been in love with Miles Carew in varying ways since she was twelve years old, and he'd been her idol. But now he'd stepped down from his pedestal with a vengeance here in this very bed only a couple of hours before. And how she wished he hadn't. Before tonight she'd had only the theory of love to languish over. Now the bliss of the interlude in his arms was etched on her memory forever.

Next morning Elinor was in luck, of a kind. When she went up to the house, tense with nerves, Mrs Hedley told her Miles was in his study with the contractors he'd engaged to build the new gymnasium in the walled garden.

'Shall I fetch him for you, Elinor?' asked the housekeeper, noting Elinor's dark-rimmed eyes. 'You look very tired, my dear. Looking after Sophie's really taken it out of you!'

'I'm fine, Mrs H,' Elinor assured her. 'And don't disturb him. It was Sophie I came to see anyway. How is she this morning?'

'A bit peaky, but a lot better. Mr Miles made her promise to stay in bed until her mother comes back this morning.' Mrs Hedley's lips tightened. 'I suppose you've heard Mrs Carew—I mean Mrs Forbes—is taking Sophie away on holiday?'

Elinor nodded. 'A spot of sunshine could be just what Sophie needs. I'll go on up, shall I?'

'Of course, dear. And when you come back down I've got some of your things packed up. I ironed them for you.'

Thanking her, Elinor left the kitchen and went quietly upstairs to the small room at the end of the landing, her heart contracting as the pale little face on the pillows lit up at the sight of her.

'Nell!' Sophie shot up and stretched out her arms, and Elinor cuddled her close.

'Hello, darling, how are you today?'

'Better.' The thin arms clutched at her. 'Nell, have you seen Jet? Is she all right?'

'She's out with Meg and Tom, playing in the garden,' Elinor assured her huskily. 'You'd better get well as quickly as you can so you can go out to play with her too.'

Sophie sat back against her pillows, looking glum. 'I can't for a while. I'm going away with Mummy tomorrow. To a place called Canaries.'

'How lovely! You'll like that; it's sunny there, and you'll come back all brown and well.'

Sophie fixed Elinor with imploring brown eyes. 'Can't you come too?'

'You won't need me when you've got Mummy, darling. But you can send me a postcard—one with a picture of your hotel on it.'

Elinor found it so painful to part with Sophie that she could hardly speak when she got back to Mrs Hedley in the kitchen. 'I'm off now, Mrs H,' she said thickly, blowing her nose. 'I'm going back to Cheltenham today so I won't see you for a while.'

The other woman frowned. 'I thought Mr Miles said you were going to help him with this new project of his.'

Elinor flushed. 'My boss in Cheltenham persuaded me to go back to him instead.'

Mrs Hedley handed her a neat parcel. 'I'm sorry to hear that, Elinor. Does Sophie know?'

Elinor shook her head miserably. 'And please don't tell her, Mrs H. By the time she comes back she'll be fit and well and better able to understand why I can't stay.'

Mrs Hedley sighed. 'I wish *I* did. I've known you since you were Sophie's age, Elinor, so you won't take offense if I say Mr Miles is going to be very upset when he finds you're off today. Are you sure I can't fetch him to talk to you?'

'No!' said Elinor in alarm. 'Please don't. You know my parents came home last night, so I must get back. Thanks a lot for doing my ironing.' She gave the woman a quick, impulsive hug. 'Good-bye, Mrs H.'

As Elinor ran down the drive a scarlet car swept in through the gate and came to a halt beside her. Selina, groomed to perfection, leaned her vivid head through the open window.

'Hello, there, you're in a hurry,' she said, smiling her white, professional smile.

'Good morning, Mrs Forbes,' returned Elinor politely, poised to run.

'Ah, so Miles told you I was married.' Selina's smile cooled. 'But don't let the news go to your head, my dear. I may be married to Lloyd, but that doesn't affect my relationship with Miles in the least.'

Elinor smiled, outwardly unmoved. 'Not really my business, Mrs Forbes.'

The blue eyes hardened. 'Very sensible of you to realise that. And just remember that, whatever legal arrangement Miles bullied me into, Sophie is *my* child.' She turned on her confident smile.

'And last but definitely not least, Miles, whatever he may say to the contrary, still carries a torch for me. If he ever does marry again, which I doubt, he'll only force himself into it for Sophie's sake.'

With that she withdrew her head, put her foot down on the accelerator and sent the car roaring up to the house. Elinor, white to the lips, forced herself to walk away without hurry, only allowing herself to run when she'd turned into the drive off Cliff Cottage. Less than two hours later she walked into the offices of Renfrew and Maynard and told Oliver she was ready to get back to work.

When she returned to the flat that evening, having refused Oliver's offer of dinner, Elinor was relieved to find that Linda had gone out for the evening. A note fastened to the refrigerator welcomed her back, told her Linda would be late, that there was ham and cheese and a new brown loaf for her supper, if fancied, and that someone called Miles Carew had called and left a number for her to call back.

Elinor crumpled the note and threw it in the bin, had a quick shower, then assembled a meal from the delicacies supplied by Linda and ate it listlessly while she went on with the thriller she'd begun centuries before in Cliff Cottage. Her concentration was somewhat less than absolute because all the time she kept expecting the telephone to ring. Since it didn't, once her meal was over she picked up the phone reluctantly and rang the number of Cliff House, both relieved and disappointed when it was Mrs Hedley who answered, not Miles.

Miles, it seemed, was dining in town with the newlyweds, and Mrs Hedley was looking after Sophie.

'How is she?'

'A lot better, but making a bit of a fuss about going off to the Canaries tomorrow. She thought Mr Miles was going too, you see.'

'Oh, dear! Is she sleeping now?'

'Yes, thank heaven. Tom's sitting with her at the moment while I pack her things. I think it's daft taking her all that way, myself.' Mrs Hedley sniffed disapprovingly. 'Your mother came and gave her the once-over this afternoon and says she's well enough to travel, though. Stayed and played snakes and ladders with her too. She's a great favourite with Sophie.'

Elinor swallowed hard. 'Mother's very fond of her. So am I. Anyway,' she went on hastily, 'tell Miles I rang. No message. I was just returning his call. An early start for me in the morning, so I'm off to bed.'

She took her book to bed, lying tense and expectant as time went by. But Miles didn't ring. She turned her tear-stained face into the pillow and tried to sleep.

It was so hectic at the offices of Renfrew and Maynard next day that she had no time for private problems, and when she got back to the flat, later than usual, Linda was there, full of confidences about her love-affair. When the telephone interrupted the flow Linda answered with her usual cheery greeting, told the caller to hang on a moment and handed the receiver to Elinor. 'For you—I'm off out. See you later.'

Elinor waved her off, took a deep breath, then said a quiet hello.

'Miles,' was the curt response. 'Elinor, what the devil are you playing at?'

'I'm not playing at anything. I just came back to work. I told you I was going to.'

'After what happened the other night I felt entitled to some kind of explanation in person before you took off,' he said bitterly.

'Why?'

'*Why?*' He breathed in audibly. 'Can you imagine how I felt when Mrs Hedley passed on your message? I went down to see your parents later, but all they could tell me was that you'd decided to go back to your job. My proposal of marriage was something they felt unable to discuss.'

'What proposal, Miles?'

'You know bloody well!'

'You haven't made one to me.'

There was a pause. 'Only,' he said coldly, 'because you took off before I could do so. You heard what I said to your parents so you knew perfectly well I'd bring the subject up the moment I saw you.' He paused again. 'Am I to assume you went chasing back to Cheltenham just to avoid seeing me?'

'I did come to see you. You were busy so I wouldn't let Mrs Hedley interrupt you. I saw Sophie, of course.'

'I know. She told me.'

'I saw Selina too.'

'Now *she* didn't tell me.'

'There wasn't much to tell.'

'Why do I find that hard to believe, I wonder? Did she say something to send you running off? A favourite pastime of yours—do you always run from problems you can't face?'

'No, I do not,' said Elinor coldly. 'It just seemed the best time to come, while Sophie was occupied with her mother and the holiday. Did she get off all right?'

'She went. But parting with her was a harrowing business.' He sounded depressed. 'I just hope Selina will take proper care of her.'

'Surely she will—it isn't for long.'

'I keep telling myself that. But a lot can happen in two weeks—even less than that in some circumstances,' he added with significance. 'Which brings me to the matter in hand. You know perfectly well I want to marry you. After the other night I thought it was a foregone conclusion. Then it struck me that Maynard thought that once too. So does this flight of yours mean that as a lover I was tried and found wanting?'

She ground her teeth. 'Is that why you rang? For reassurance on your performance?'

'You know damn well it isn't. I wanted to come chasing after you tonight, now Sophie's gone, but I'm coming down with a cold or some damn thing so I took your mother's advice and left you to yourself for a while. Which doesn't mean I've changed my mind. Hell, Elinor, it isn't as though we met for the first time that night in the snow. We've known each other for years.' He sighed irritably. 'Look, I'd rather not propose down a telephone wire, but under the circumstances I haven't got much choice. Will you marry me, Elinor?'

Ignoring the urge to scream yes, Elinor said, very quietly, 'No, Miles, I won't.'

There was a pause. 'Would you mind telling me why?' he said at last, equally quiet.

She took a deep breath. 'To put it in a nutshell, Miles, you're asking me to marry you for the wrong reasons. You just want a mother for Sophie. And one way and another I seem tailor-made to your requirements: someone who loves Sophie, willing to help with your project, happy to live in quiet Stavely, a restful companion for the long winter evenings and—the icing on the cake—someone you quite fancy in your bed now you've tried me out. Who else could fill the bill so perfectly?'

'You're angry,' he concluded.

Elinor blinked back sudden, unwelcome tears. 'I don't know why,' she admitted thickly. 'I mean, it's so convenient, isn't it? I'm not even required to move house.'

'You're crying! Elinor, please don't. Lord, this is a bloody stupid way to propose. If I were there I could take you in my arms and show you why you should say yes.'

'It wouldn't work,' she said flatly, sniffing. 'There's more to marriage than that side of it. I should have thought you, of all people, should know that.'

'Ah. Is it my lack of success with Selina that's sticking in your throat, by any chance?' he said swiftly. 'Did she say something to you this morning?'

'Nothing of any importance.'

'Whatever it was didn't do me much good.' He coughed, and cleared his throat impatiently. 'Your parents don't object, by the way. They gave me their blessing. Which, unfortunately, isn't much use without a yes from you. I suppose it's no use reminding you how delighted Sophie would be if you agreed?'

'Miles,' said Elinor coolly, 'I'm very fond of Sophie, and I wouldn't knowingly do anything to hurt her. But I can't marry you just to provide her with another mother. She already has one. Selina reminded me of that this morning.'

'I might have known!' He swore softly. 'But Sophie isn't the only reason, Nell.'

'Other than wanting a mother for Sophie, would you mind telling me exactly why you do want to marry me?' demanded Elinor.

'Why do I get the feeling this is some kind of test? One I'll probably fail, at that!'

She said nothing, waiting pointedly for him to go on.

'All right,' he began slowly. 'As you seem to re-member so vividly, I once told you I fell in love with Selina, and one experience like that was enough. Since that time my career and my child have taken up my entire attention. To be honest, if it weren't for Sophie I wouldn't have resigned from the army. But because she was my priority I did.

'Then you erupted into my life that night and showed me just what was lacking in it. Not just sex, though that was undeniably part of it, but companionship, a feeling of rapport I'd never experienced with a woman before. I wouldn't have chosen the situation which threw us together, but almost from the start I was glad of it because it meant we were together day and night. And all too soon I wanted more than just companionship. Any red-blooded man would, thrown together like that with you, Nell. I couldn't help marvelling over the transformation from the cute little urchin I used to know. Elinor Gibson grown-up was someone I liked a lot. Exactly how much I discovered when I thought you'd fallen over the cliff.'

He paused and Elinor waited, hardly daring to breathe.

'Since Sophie soon felt the same way,' he continued, 'it seemed like a natural progression. You'd finished with your relationship, and there were Sophie and I, both in crying need of you here with us. My own need I demonstrated the other night, rather sooner than I meant to. So there you have my reasons for wanting to marry you. Are they enough to make you say yes?'

Shattering disappointment kept her silent for so long that Miles said at last, 'Obviously not.'

'Perhaps I'm just off the thought of marriage,' she said woodenly. 'For now, at least.'

'Does that mean you may eventually look on it in a more favourable light? Or merely that I'm not the right candidate?' he demanded.

'Just that I need time to myself to think, I suppose, Miles. I haven't really had much time for that since I ran from Oliver in the snow.'

'And fell out of the frying-pan into the fire!'

Oh, yes, thought Elinor, clenching her teeth. She couldn't have put it better. 'I hope Sophie enjoys her holiday,' she went on. 'Give her my love when you talk to her and tell her I'll come and visit her when she gets back.'

'She doesn't know you've gone away,' he said grimly. 'She thought you were spending time with your mummy and daddy. I hadn't the heart to say you'd deserted her.'

'I *haven't* deserted her,' cried Elinor hotly. 'I deliberately chose a good time to go—when she was with her mother. Stop trying to make me feel guilty, Miles!'

'Something tells me I don't have to try. I know you well.'

He didn't know her that well, she thought bitterly, or he'd have known exactly what he'd left off his rotten list. All he had to say was 'I love you, Elinor', and she'd be rushing back to Stavely right this minute.

'I must go,' she said wearily. 'I'm flattered you want to marry me, and I hope we'll always be——'

'Good friends?' His voice stabbed the words down the line. 'I want a whole lot more than that, Elinor, as you know very well. I want you in my bed, as well as helping me take care of Sophie. If friendship is all you can offer, keep it for my daughter. I'm not interested. Goodbye.'

Elinor put the receiver down and turned blindly, tripping over a rug on her way to her room. She threw herself down on the bed in tears, cursing herself for the stupid pride which wouldn't let her accept the nearest thing to her heart's desire she was ever likely to be offered.

CHAPTER ELEVEN

AT THE end of a week without any further word from Miles Elinor resigned herself to the fact that he'd meant what he'd said. Her hopes had soared when she had come home one evening to find that a great basket of flowers had arrived for her. Linda had waited eagerly while Elinor had taken the accompanying card from its envelope, then sighed, disappointed.

'Obviously not from the man you're agonising over, then.'

'Afraid not,' Elinor had said brightly. 'They're from someone I met in Stavely when I went home.'

'Nice?'

'Not my cup of tea at all, actually. Nice thought, though.'

The flowers, to her surprise, were from Alexander Reid and the card, which she had kept firmly away from Linda's curious eyes, expressed his sorrow and remorse for the episode at Cliff House. For a moment she'd been sure the flowers were from Miles, and her disappointment was so intense she'd have thrown them away if it hadn't been for the inevitable explanations to Linda.

With Cliff Cottage barred to her as a bolt-hole to lick her wounds this time she asked her parents to stay at the flat for the weekend instead. Linda was spending it with Josh, and the prospect of two days of her own undiluted company held no appeal for Elinor. Her father, however, was filling in as locum at the practice in Stavely while one of his former colleagues was on holiday and was on call over the weekend—so much for retirement! Elinor thought wryly—so Mrs Gibson drove to Cheltenham to spend Friday evening with her.

'I thought you might have come home this weekend,' she said on arrival. 'While we're still at Cliff Cottage.'

Elinor sighed. 'Nothing I'd have liked better. But under the circumstances it's best I keep out of the way. Have you seen Miles lately?' she couldn't help adding.

'Your father has. The builders made a start on the alterations this week, so things are fairly hectic up there.'

'I've had a postcard from Sophie.' Elinor fetched a brightly coloured card, with a painstakingly printed message to the effect that Sophie was better, missed Jet and sent her love to Nell. 'How is Jet?' she asked.

'Growing fast—but Meg keeps her in hand, and Tom Hedley's marvellous with dogs, of course. She's house-trained now.'

'Does Miles take her for walks?'

'I haven't seen him doing so lately, but Tom sees she gets plenty of exercise.' Mrs Gibson eyed her daughter closely. 'I've seen you look better, darling. Are you eating properly?'

Elinor nodded. 'Quite well, actually. Linda's a great cook.'

'You'll miss her when she moves in with this Josh of hers. What will you do then? Advertise for another flatmate?'

'I thought I'd try and manage on my own for a bit. Oliver gave me a rise when I went back, so it should be possible.' She gave her mother a wry smile. 'It hardly seems fair to ask some stranger to put up with my company at the moment.'

'How does Linda cope?'

Elinor smiled. 'She's so much in love at the moment nothing troubles her—she's walking on air.'

'While you're so much in love you're down in the depths,' observed Mrs Gibson casually.

Elinor stared at her mother, the colour draining from her face. 'Is it so obvious?' she said bitterly.

'To me it is.' Mary Gibson leaned across the table and put her hand on Elinor's. 'Look, darling, Miles told us he'd done his best to persuade you to say yes to his proposal, yet you turned him down. I hate to see you unhappy like this. Is there no possibility you'll change your mind?'

'If Miles had tried again, or come to see me, maybe I'd have pocketed my pride, decided to take the package he offered and tried to forget the fact that he doesn't love me.' She stared at her mother miserably. 'But I haven't heard a word from him since that night.'

Mrs Gibson sighed. 'Oh, dear—I'm not supposed to tell you this—medical ethics and all that, not to mention the fact that Miles swore me to silence...'

'What do you *mean*? What's the matter?' demanded Elinor in alarm.

'Nothing drastic. Miles came down with Sophie's flu after he spoke to you, that's all. And like all fit, healthy men he's been an absolute pain as an invalid. You'd think it was a crime to be ill. The poor Hedleys have had their work cut out trying to keep him in bed.

Your father's been to see him most days because he proved to be allergic to the antibiotics prescribed for his chest infection.'

'Chest infection?' said Elinor in alarm.

'Yes. Perfectly normal side-effect of flu, child. Anyway Miles was quite ill for a few days——'

'Why on earth didn't you tell me?' Elinor cut in fiercely.

'Because he asked us not to.' Mrs Gibson sighed. 'I'm only telling you now because I can't bear to see that look on your face. Besides, even if Miles hadn't been ill, I don't know how you expected him to keep ringing you if you'd turned him down. Miles is a proud man, Elinor. A woman's walked out on him once already, remember. A second rejection can't have been easy for him.'

'It's a thought that's been haunting me,' admitted Elinor guiltily. 'Time and time again I've picked up the phone and put it down again.'

'I've a better suggestion,' said her mother briskly. 'Come back with me tonight.'

Elinor swallowed. 'You mean go and see him?'

'Not if you don't want to. But Sophie's due back in the morning, and frankly Miles is in no condition to cope with her at the moment, so I suggested she stay at Cliff Cottage until he's up and about. You could be a big help. If you want to,' added Mrs Gibson unnecessarily as her daughter shot off to her bedroom to pack.

Elinor found it hard to sleep in the familiar bed in her old bedroom that night, knowing Miles was only a short distance away at Cliff House. Which wasn't the only reason. Just being here in the same bed where he'd made love to her so fiercely scotched any hope of a night's rest. After tossing and turning for hours she got up early and dressed, then crept quietly down to the kitchen to find her father just returning from a call.

'Hello, Dad—you look tired. Like some tea?'

Dr Gibson yawned. 'Several pints of it, I think. Mrs Hawkins thought she was having a heart attack again. As usual it was indigestion. A dose of her mixture and she was right as rain.'

Elinor poured water into the teapot. 'Shall I cook some bacon and eggs?'

'Heart attack on a plate?' He grinned. 'Not much use scolding Mrs Hawkins for her death-wish diet if I follow her example. Just a couple of slices of nice healthy wholemeal toast will do fine.'

'How's Miles, Dad?' asked Elinor as she sliced bread.

'I called in last night after your mother drove to see you. He's a lot better, but definitely not up to coping with young Sophie for a bit.'

'Will she be able to see him?'

'Yes, of course; don't want to worry the child. But I've laid the law down. He's not to get up yet, so she can just pay him a visit then come back here with us.'

Elinor couldn't bring herself to ask if she could visit Miles too. She sat down at the kitchen table with her father, chattered about the building going on next door and asked if everything was going smoothly with the purchase of the house in Monmouth.

'Look,' said her father, seeing through her, 'if you want to see Miles, the best thing is to ask first. He's been feeling pretty rough. He may not fancy a visit from anyone—except Sophie—for the time being.'

'Including the new Mrs Forbes?' said Elinor acidly.

'Selina?' Her father snorted. 'She's not even coming back with Sophie—too exhausted. I gather the bridegroom cometh to deliver his stepdaughter. He's driving her down this morning.'

Elinor pulled a face. 'I'll keep out of the way. I'll ring Mrs H presently and ask her to send Sophie down with Tom whenever she wants to come.'

After making the call later, with an affectionate greeting for Mrs Hedley and a polite, careful inquiry about Miles, Elinor spent the morning curled up on the window-seat of her bedroom where she had an uninterrupted view of any visitors to Cliff House. It was almost midday before a large, unfamiliar car swept in through the gates, with Sophie on the back seat.

'She's arrived,' cried Elinor, running downstairs to her mother in the kitchen.

'She'll take a while for her reunion with Miles and the Hedleys, not to mention the puppy, so I won't make a start on lunch until she gets here,' said Mrs Gibson, and smiled. 'I had a job to persuade Mrs H to let us feed Sophie here.'

Elinor grinned spontaneously for the first time in days. 'A good thing you won. No chance of burgers at Cliff House!'

Elinor was unprepared for her feeling of joy as the small figure in a bright pink tracksuit came flying up the drive to the cottage with Jet on the lead, Tom Hedley panting behind with a suitcase.

'Nell, Nell,' shrieked the child, dropping Jet's lead, and threw herself into Elinor's arms. The puppy streaked through into the kitchen with Tom in hot, apologetic pursuit, and the Gibsons stood laughing,

Mrs Gibson rather moist about the eyes as she watched the reunion between her daughter and Sophie Carew.

'Gosh, you're brown!' said Elinor, blinking hard as she smiled down at Sophie when she let her go at last. 'Did you have a lovely time?'

Sophie wrinkled her nose. 'It was OK, but I missed you and Daddy a lot. *I* thought Daddy was going too. But it was only Lloyd,' she added with scorn.

'And Mummy,' Elinor reminded her, as they went into the kitchen.

'Mummy had lots of headaches,' said Sophie, shrugging, 'so I played with some other children every day. They had their nanny with them.'

'Well, that was nice,' said Mrs Gibson brightly, taking the suitcase from Tom Hedley.

'Is it all right if the puppy stays here, Dr Gibson?' he asked her. 'Sophie didn't want to leave her behind.'

Once a reassured Tom had departed Dr Gibson went off to read his paper with a peaceful sherry, his wife began to cook lunch and Elinor took Sophie's suitcase up to the spare room, the child at her heels chattering nineteen to the dozen.

'I sleep in the room opposite,' said Elinor as they unpacked the case, 'so if you want me all you have to do is call.'

'I love this house,' said Sophie happily. 'Soon Daddy's bringing me to live here forever and ever. Can't you stay and live here too, Nell?'

'There'll be no room for me once the Hedleys move in as well,' said Elinor, hanging up sweaters and jeans in the wardrobe.

Sophie bounced gently on the bed, looking surprised. 'They're not coming. Only Daddy and me. They're going to stay at Cliff House.'

'Oh. I see.' Elinor sat down on the bed and put her arm round Sophie, looking down into the suntanned little face. 'Darling, I have a home of my own, you know, in Cheltenham, where I work. But I'll come and see you as often as I can, I promise.'

The small mouth quivered. 'I wish you'd stay here with us, Nell.'

Elinor hugged her close. 'I can't, darling. But perhaps Daddy will let you come and spend weekends with me, and we'll go shopping and go to the cinema——'

'Have you and Daddy quarrelled?' interrupted Sophie accusingly. 'He's had flu, like me. Have you been to see him?'

Elinor cleared her throat. 'Well, no, not yet, Sophie. I thought it best to ask first if he feels like visitors. How is he?'

'He's in bed,' said Sophie anxiously. 'He's getting up this afternoon. I'm going back to see him. Will you come too?'

Elinor chose her words with care. 'You visit him first, and ask him if he feels well enough to see me. Perhaps he'd prefer to rest.'

'Course he'll want to see you,' said Sophie scornfully, and slid off the bed, sniffing the air. 'I'm hungry.'

After lunch Elinor suggested a walk in the spring sunshine, and took Sophie off with Jet to roam all over the gardens of Cliff House, Sophie having been assured that Meg would probably be grateful to be left in peace.

'Oh, look,' said Sophie suddenly, waving madly. 'There's Daddy at his bedroom window.'

Elinor's heart leapt to her throat. 'So it is,' she said brightly, after a swift glance. 'Let's take Jet back to the cottage, then you can come back here and go up and see him.'

She stayed with Mrs Hedley in the kitchen at Cliff House later, while Sophie dashed upstairs like a whirlwind.

'What a difference,' said the housekeeper indulgently. 'I don't mind telling you, Elinor, I had my doubts about her going all that way straight on top of flu. But it looks as though the sunshine did her good.'

'Apparently she made friends with some other children and their nanny.'

Mrs Hedley sniffed in unspoken disapproval.

'How *is* Miles now?' Elinor couldn't help asking.

'Better, but he hasn't been too clever, and that's a fact.' Mrs Hedley looked her visitor in the eye. 'He was in a right old tear when he found you'd gone. If he hadn't been feeling so bad I think he'd have come after you—we had a terrible job to persuade him to go to bed. Then the pills he got for his chest made him worse—thank goodness your father was just next door.'

Sophie came into the room, looking disconsolate. 'Daddy says he'd like some tea when you've got time, Mrs Hedley.'

'Right away, my lovely.' Mrs Hedley went off to fill the kettle immediately, and Elinor looked at the little girl questioningly.

'Did you remember to ask Daddy if he wanted to see me, Sophie?'

Sophie nodded, her mouth drooping. 'He said he wasn't fit for visitors yet. Only me.'

Elinor breathed in shakily. 'Of course. Perfectly understandable. Flu's a nasty thing—you ought to know, Miss Carew! Come on, let's take Jet back and give poor Meg some peace. Bye, Mrs Hedley.'

The sympathy in the other woman's eyes almost had her in tears as she shepherded Sophie and the puppy outside, feeling the rejection like a physical pain.

Elinor went back to Cheltenham early on the Monday morning, after a rather tearful parting from Sophie, who, even with her father much improved and able to have her back at Cliff House, was deeply reluctant to part with her.

'I'll come back on Friday evening,' promised Elinor, hugging her close. 'Then we can spend some time together over the weekend—if Daddy agrees.'

In the train on the way back she stared blindly through the window at the passing vista of sunlit fields, still finding it hard to accept that Miles Carew, while now fit enough to play with his daughter and receive purely social visits from Dr Henry Gibson, still vetoed any visit from Dr Gibson's daughter. He could hardly make things clearer, thought Elinor despondently. He'd had his revenge. Tit for tat. One rejection for another. Perhaps his pride was appeased now.

She tried hard to make herself angry with him, but it was useless. Even now, when she was actually on her way back to Cheltenham, she could hardly believe she'd spent the weekend at Cliff Cottage without seeing Miles, other than as a fleeting shadow at his bedroom window.

In an effort to adjust to life without Miles, Elinor accepted when Oliver asked her to have dinner with him a couple of days later.

'No strings,' he assured her. 'Just your company for a meal.'

As an alternative to another evening alone in the flat it was attractive. Unfortunately, however, Elinor's mood was a trifle abstracted. In her misery about Miles she forgot to pay her usual attention to what she chose to eat, and by the time Oliver drove her home she was doubled up with stomach pains and felt hideously queasy.

'My God,' said Oliver in alarm as he helped her up the steps to the front door. 'It's not appendix, is it?'

'No,' gasped Elinor, handing him her key. 'There must have been onions in something.'

'Oh, hell!' He half dragged her up the stairs to her flat. 'I'd forgotten your allergy. I never thought to check when you ordered that rice thing.'

'Neither did I,' she said bitterly, and turned at the door, trying to smile. 'Sorry, Oliver, can't invite you in—I feel like death.'

'Of course not, dear girl. Don't come in tomorrow. Have a day in bed,' he implored her, and beat a hasty retreat.

Elinor smiled a little in spite of the pain. Oliver wasn't at his best around sick-rooms. Rather like Selina, really. Only nicer. She spent a night of familiar pain and discomfort, knowing of old that there was nothing to be done other than endure until the next day. When she staggered, pallid-faced, into the kitchen next morning Linda was there, looking depressingly blooming as she made a pot of tea.

'Lord, El, you look ghastly! Hangover?'

'Onions,' said Elinor succinctly.

'Oh, bad luck; are you any better now? Want something to eat?'

Elinor shook her head. 'No, thanks, but I'll have some tea now—if you'll pour it out. I don't think I could lift the teapot.'

Once she was alone she got herself back to bed and stayed there, with the radio for company and several books and, eventually, another offering of flowers—from Oliver this time, with a get-well card. Later she rang her mother and reported on the onion attack.

'I forgot to check when I ordered this risotto thing,' she said sheepishly.

'Elinor! What were you thinking of?'

'You know perfectly well what I was thinking of!' said Elinor, and burst into tears. 'Sorry—Mother—I shouldn't have rung to tell you,' she gasped, sniffing hard. 'Because as you well know, Doctor, there's not a blind thing you can do.'

'Have you taken some of your medicine?'

'Yes. Actually I'm better now. The worst part was overnight. Anyway I'm OK, but I'm going to try to get to sleep early, which is why I'm ringing now. Is Sophie all right?'

'Yes, bright as a button.' Mrs Gibson paused. 'Miles is better too. I saw him today—in a purely social capacity. He came to thank me for having Sophie over the weekend.'

'Did he mention me?'

'No, darling. He was only here a moment or two. Now he's up and about again there's a lot to do with the new project.'

Elinor scrubbed at her eyes. 'I'm sure there must be. Time I got back to my bed of pain, I think. Good night, Mother—give my love to Sophie and tell her I'll see her on Friday.'

She went back to work next day feeling a bit fragile, but otherwise none the worse for wear after her run-in with the risotto, much to Oliver's relief. Nevertheless she felt more tired than usual when she got back to the flat, and a glance in the bathroom mirror told her she was looking rather less than her best. Linda had gone off for the rest of the week to help Josh decorate the new flat and Elinor was glad of the quiet. She had a bath, wrapped herself in her towelling robe, dried her hair, then opened a tin of mushroom soup, made some toast, and propped a book against the teapot so that she could read while she ate.

The intercom buzzed halfway through the meal, and with a sigh of irritation she took the receiver from the wall.

'Yes?'

'Elinor?'

Her sorely tried stomach muscles tied in knots.

'Elinor?' repeated the voice urgently. 'It's Miles.'

Did he think she didn't recognise his voice? 'What do you want?' she said ungraciously.

'To see you, of course,' he answered in kind, then paused. 'I won't take up much of your time.'

Breathing in deeply a few times to calm herself, Elinor pressed the release button, then went to the door. She watched Miles coming up the stairs, and her heart turned over. He was haggard, and thinner, and there were dark marks under his eyes, but he looked elegant and self-contained as ever in a tweed jacket and the cords and desert boots he seemed to live in most of the time, and it took every ounce of self-control she possessed not to throw herself into his arms.

'Hello, Elinor,' he said as he reached her.

'Hello, Miles,' she said without warmth. 'What a surprise. Are you better?'

He nodded. 'May I come in?'

'Of course.' She ushered him into the sitting-room. 'I was just eating my supper. Can I offer you anything?'

'No, thanks; I can't stay long.'

'Then perhaps you'll come into the kitchen while I finish my meal.' This was sheer bravado. One look at Miles had killed any desire to eat. He sat down on the chair she indicated, then looked at her across the small table as she picked up her spoon.

'Your mother told me you'd been...unwell. Stomach trouble. You look very pale. Have you seen a doctor?'

She smiled faintly. 'I've got two at home, remember.'

He unbent sufficiently to return the smile. 'Of course. Stupid of me.'

Elinor gave up any pretence of eating and got up to put her dishes in the sink. 'My capacity's still limited, I'm afraid, but I've just made tea. Would you like some? Or there's a beer in the fridge.'

'Tea will be fine.'

She busied herself with pouring tea in cups, and adding milk. 'So what brings you to Cheltenham?' she asked politely, since Miles seemed disinclined to break the silence.

'I'd have thought it was obvious. I came to see you.'

'Why? You refused the privilege last weekend.'

'I know,' he said quietly. 'But that was before I heard.'

'Heard what?'

'Don't play games, Elinor; you know damn well what I'm talking about,' he said impatiently.

'I do *not*.' She glared at him. 'Unless you've come to gloat because you've paid me back!'

He frowned. 'Paid you back?'

'This is ridiculous.' She jumped up, tightening the belt of her dressing-gown. 'It's a bit chilly in here.'

'You can say that again!' he snapped, getting to his feet.

'I meant,' she went on with dignity, 'that it's warmer in the other room.' She marched out of the kitchen, head high, and went into the sitting-room to curl up in her usual chair. 'Please shut the door and sit down,' she said, waving a hand at the sofa.

'What did you mean about paying you back?' he asked, sitting erect.

Elinor shrugged. 'When you refused to see me last weekend I took it as some form of retaliation on your part—for not accepting your offer.'

'It was a proposal, not an offer,' he said cuttingly. 'And it's obvious your opinion of me must be pretty low if you think I'd be so petty. If you want the truth I felt like hell, looked like hell, and in my male vanity wanted to appear rather more presentable before I saw you. Sophie told me you were coming home again on Friday. I'd hoped to look more human by then.'

'I see,' said Elinor without expression. So Miles was subject to vanity like lesser mortals, after all. She looked at him levelly. 'If you already knew I'd be back in Stavely on Friday why have you come here tonight?'

'Because I couldn't wait until then to see if my suspicions were correct.'

Suspicions? What did he think she'd been doing?

'And,' he went on, before she could speak, 'it was hardly a subject to discuss on the phone.'

'I see,' she said again. 'Or rather I don't see. What's all this about suspicions?'

'Think about it!'

'I am thinking,' she retorted, baffled. 'But I still haven't a clue what you're talking about.'

'The episode in your bedroom a while back may have slipped your mind entirely by this time,' said Miles savagely, 'but I'm haunted by it. I can't stop thinking about how we were together. Bloody stupid, isn't it?'

'Not at all.'

His eyes locked with hers. 'You mean you think about it too?'

Her pallid face burned with sudden colour. 'Of course I do! But——'

'But you still insist you don't know what I'm worried about?' he demanded. 'Your mother said you were ill, some stomach bug or other——'

'No——' began Elinor, but he brushed her interruption aside.

'I could hardly come right out with it and ask her if stomach bug was a polite euphemism for something else entirely!' he said urgently.

Elinor gazed at him in sudden enlightenment. 'Did my mother really say stomach bug?'

He frowned. 'Not in so many words. I suppose she might have said an upset, or something. I took it that she meant a stomach bug.'

'Miles,' said Elinor quietly, 'I did something very silly the other night—went out to dinner and didn't check on the ingredients in the risotto I ate. It had onions in it, which had the usual horrible effect. But I am not pregnant, if that's what's brought on this rush of solicitude.'

'You're sure?' he rapped out.

'Of course I am! I've been sure since a few days after—after that night,' she added awkwardly, then looked at him curiously. 'That's a very strange look on your face, Miles. Could it be relief?'

He jumped to his feet and stood glaring down at her. 'Like hell it is! Can't you recognise disappointment when you see it? If you were expecting my child I'd have made you marry me.'

'Nothing could *make* me marry anyone unless I chose to,' she said with hauteur. 'Besides,' she added with calculated cruelty, 'even if I had been pregnant how could you have known the child was yours?'

Miles paled so visibly that she jumped to her feet and took his arm.

'I didn't mean it,' she said with a rush of contrition. 'You hurt me so much when you refused to see me. I wanted to hit back—I'm only human.'

'So am I,' he muttered, and pulled her into his arms so that she stood off balance. 'And if this is the only way I can get through to you...' He bent his head and kissed her, and Elinor kissed him back, the first touch of his mouth showing her beyond all doubt that the precise nature of his feelings was an irrelevance as long as he wanted her like this.

'It doesn't matter any more,' she gasped against his mouth as he sat down with her in his lap.

'What doesn't?' he muttered, his lips moving down her throat, and she shivered. He asked if she was cold and she showed him she wasn't, and he laid her back against the cushions, his hands sliding between the lapels of her robe to find her breasts, his mouth smothering the explanations which swiftly dwindled in importance until Elinor couldn't imagine how she'd ever denied Miles Carew anything it was in her power to give.

'Oh, God, I forgot,' he said in anguish after a while, the breath tearing through his chest. 'You've been ill.'

'So have you,' she gasped, wriggling closer.

'I'm in sore need of some medicine,' he agreed hoarsely, and kissed her again. 'And only you can provide it, darling—administered at regular intervals for the rest of my life.'

'Is this malady of yours catching?' she demanded, smiling at him with such radiance that his eyes narrowed as though dazzled.

'Lord, I hope so,' he said fervently, and kissed her again with renewed urgency. 'Why did you turn me down, darling? Not that it makes a blind bit of difference. I'm going to marry you if I have to carry you into church over my shoulder.'

Elinor, quite enchanted by the picture this conjured up, returned his kisses with such fervour that it was some time before Miles released her to demand an answer.

'It was your list of reasons,' she said, gasping for breath.

He groaned. 'Not that blasted list again! I've never tried so much persuasion in my life, and still it didn't work.'

'You left something off,' she said baldly.

He raised his head to look down at her flushed, damp face. 'What was it?'

'You didn't say you loved me—and please, Miles,' she said in a rush, 'it doesn't matter any more. I know you care for me, and . . . well, it's obvious you want me . . .'

'Elinor,' he said sternly. 'Are you telling me you turned me down because you think I don't love you?'

She let out a great quivering sigh, nodding dumbly.

He jumped to his feet and tore off his jacket, then lay full-length beside her on the sofa, his eyes gazing deep into hers. 'Then what did you think I meant when you went over the cliff? I thought I made it clear that I felt as if half of me had torn away and fallen with you. Why do you think I half killed Sandy Reid?'

'But you never said it in so many words, Miles,' she whispered.

'I suppose it never occurred to me that I needed to.'

'You bet you needed to,' she told him crossly. 'If you had you could have saved us both a lot of trouble. Besides,' she added, burying her face against his shoulder, 'Selina seemed so confident you still fancied her.'

'Selina needs to think all men fancy her, my darling.' Miles laughed suddenly. 'Have you heard Sophie's account of the holiday, by the way?'

'You mean having a fun time with somebody else's children and their nanny?' Elinor sniffed.

'I had a word with the new Mrs Forbes over the phone,' he said grimly. 'I told her if that was the best she could do Sophie was better left with me, other than the occasional day out.'

'But she is Sophie's mother,' said Elinor, trying to be fair.

'Only through the accident of birth. I'm not saying Selina doesn't love Sophie in her own way, but she prefers motherhood in theory. When it comes to sticking plasters on bloody knees and getting up in the night to a sick child, Selina likes to delegate.' He put a finger under Elinor's chin and turned her face up to his. 'Sophie loves her mother, naturally enough. But she loves you too, Nell. *And*—are you paying attention?—so do I. So for pity's sake stop all this shilly-shallying and marry me.'

'Is that an order, Major?' she asked, smiling.

'If I say yes, do I take it you'll obey?' he asked, winding a strand of her hair round his finger.

Elinor raised an eyebrow. 'As long as it's understood that this is a one-off. For all future dealings together, Miles Carew, I require requests, not orders.'

'Agreed!' He traced a caressing finger over her lips, then sighed. 'If I start kissing you I'll be lost. I should be making a move.'

'It's early yet,' she protested.

'If I stay you know what might happen ...'

'I was rather counting on it.'

'Oh, in that case!' He kissed her hard, then raised his head. 'A sudden thought. Is your flatmate likely to come in for a girlie chat any time soon? After the episode with your parents I confess to a certain sensitivity on the subject.'

Elinor giggled. 'Linda's staying with Josh—painting the walls in the new flat.'

'Useful girl,' said Miles. 'Are you good with a paintbrush?'

'Hopeless.'

'Pity. Never mind, you've got other attributes. You're a delight to look at, marvellous with Sophie, you can cook, you're brave and resourceful in a crisis. *But*,' he added with sudden emphasis, 'I wouldn't care if you were none of those things. I just can't live without you.'

She gazed up into his eyes, secretly flooded with joy as she listened to the words she'd given up hope of hearing him say. But instead of melting into his arms, as every instinct urged her to, she gave him a very unloverlike dig in the ribs. 'I just wish you'd said that a whole lot sooner, Miles Carew. I don't know that I should give in to you so easily. I think I'll change my mind—keep you waiting for your answer.'

He smiled slowly and pulled her close, his mouth a fraction away from hers. 'If you do I'll carry you out of here—ignoring any kicking and screaming—and take you back to Cliff House and shut you up in my bedroom until you say yes. When it comes to laying siege, Elinor Gibson, I warn you now, I'm a lot more dangerous than Alexander Reid. I won't let you out until you give in.'

'No food?'

'Maybe the odd sandwich or two.' He kissed her lingeringly. 'And of course I'll lock myself up with you and make love to you until I get my way.'

Elinor smiled radiantly and locked her arms round his neck. 'I do admire your strategy, Major. You give me no choice. But if I do say yes right now, could you carry out the siege just the same? It's a great idea for a honeymoon!'

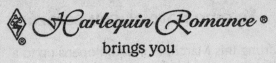

Harlequin Romance ®

brings you

How the West was Wooed!

We've rounded up twelve of our most popular authors,
and the result is a whole year of romance, Western
style. Every month we'll be bringing you a spirited,
independent woman whose heart is about to be lassoed
by a rugged, handsome, one-hundred-percent cowboy!
Watch for...

- March: **CLANTON'S WOMAN**—Patricia Knoll

- April: **A DANGEROUS MAGIC**—Patricia Wilson

- May: **THE BADLANDS BRIDE**—Rebecca Winters

- June: **RUNAWAY WEDDING**—Ruth Jean Dale

- July: **A RANCH, A RING AND EVERYTHING**—Val Daniels

Yo amo novelas con corazón!

Starting this March, Harlequin opens up to a whole new world of readers with two new romance lines in SPANISH!

Harlequin Deseo
* passionate, sensual and exciting stories

Harlequin Bianca
* romances that are fun, fresh and very contemporary

With four titles a month, each line will offer the same wonderfully romantic stories that you've come to love—now available in Spanish.

Look for them at selected retail outlets.

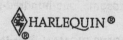

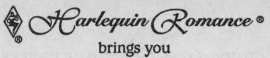

Harlequin Romance ®

brings you

HOLDING HER★
OUT FOR A

Some men are worth waiting for!

They're handsome, they're charming but, best of all, they're single! Twelve lucky women are about to discover that finding Mr. Right is not a problem—it's holding on to him.

In March the series continues with

#3401 THE ONLY MAN FOR MAGGIE
by Leigh Michaels

Karr Elliot wanted Maggie off his property but not out of his life. But Maggie didn't want a man—she wanted her own apartment!

Hold out for Harlequin Romance's heroes in coming months...

- April: THE RIGHT KIND OF MAN—Jessica Hart

- May: MOVING IN WITH ADAM—Jeanne Allan

- June: THE PARENT TRAP—Leigh Michaels

UNLOCK THE DOOR TO GREAT ROMANCE AT BRIDE'S BAY RESORT

Join Harlequin's new across-the-lines series, set in an exclusive hotel on an island off the coast of South Carolina.

Seven of your favorite authors will bring you exciting stories about fascinating heroes and heroines discovering love at Bride's Bay Resort.

Look for these fabulous stories coming to a store near you beginning in January 1996.

Harlequin American Romance #613 in January
Matchmaking Baby by Cathy Gillen Thacker

Harlequin Presents #1794 in February
Indiscretions by Robyn Donald

Harlequin Intrigue #362 in March
Love and Lies by Dawn Stewardson

Harlequin Romance #3404 in April
Make Believe Engagement by Day Leclaire

Harlequin Temptation #588 in May
Stranger in the Night by Roseanne Williams

Harlequin Superromance #695 in June
Married to a Stranger by Connie Bennett

Harlequin Historicals #324 in July
Dulcie's Gift by Ruth Langan

Visit Bride's Bay Resort each month wherever Harlequin books are sold.

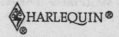

BBAYG

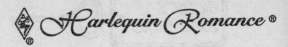

Harlequin Romance ®

New from Harlequin Romance
a very special six-book series by

MIDNIGHT SONS

DEBBIE MACOMBER

The town of Hard Luck, Alaska, needs women!

The O'Halloran brothers, who run a bush-plane service
called Midnight Sons, are heading a campaign to
attract women to Hard Luck. *(Location: north of the
Arctic Circle. Population: 150—mostly men!)*

"Debbie Macomber's *Midnight Sons* series is a delightful
romantic saga. And each book is a powerful, engaging story
in its own right. Unforgettable!"

—Linda Lael Miller

TITLE IN THE MIDNIGHT SONS SERIES: